A Chicken Was There Also

Tales of the Courageous Chickens Who Were There Through the Civil War and the Rebuilding of America

A.A. Davenport

the barrel hit a boulder and broke into a million pieces. That old man got to his feet and stumbled away, the Clary's Grove Boys laughed and heckled him. They're my heroes.

My least favorite person in New Salem is the new shop clerk my mister hired to run the place. He looks strong, but I'm pretty sure he's nothing more than a pigeon-livered horn-swoggler. He's so tall his pants are too short and he doesn't drink beer and roll dice with all the other young men of the village. Worst of all, all he does all day is read! Reading is the biggest waste of time, chickens never read. What if a tasty grasshopper hops by but you're so busy reading you never even see it? Folks around here seem to like the clerk though; they say he's honest. One time he even ran for miles to catch up to a wagon because he accidentally shortchanged a customer. What a waste of energy! If the customer didn't notice he didn't get the right change, then that's HIS fault, the clerk should have put it in his pocket and gone on with his day! These are all definitely some of the clerk's shortcomings, but my biggest problem with the clerk is that he can't seem to mind his own business where bullying is concerned.

The other day I was out in the yard and a young pullet decided to scratch around right near me. Well, she very enthusiastically scratched some dirt straight into my eyes, so I attacked her with my signature move. All chickens peck and we can sure peck hard when we want to, but I don't just peck, I bite. I like to grab a hold of a hen by the feathers of her neck. I hold on tight, shake her a few times, and give a mighty yank, slamming her to the ground. Works every time. Then, since I've proved that no one should dare mess with me, I just walk away. Well, that nosy clerk saw me do this to another hen and he scolded me! I'm not sure what all he said, but the tone of his voice was angry and I could tell he didn't approve of the way I treated that young pullet. I answered him back by putting up a fuss, I cackled so loud that even the rooster came running. I let that clerk know that his opinion wasn't welcome. Now if a tough fellow like Jack Armstrong or one of those other Clary's Grove Boys would have scolded me, I probably would have at least listened, but not that namby-pamby clerk who thinks he's something. Yes, I definitely thought Abraham Lincoln was a bit of a blockhead, that is, until I saw him fight.

Lots of the young men fight around here, it's something they do for sport and entertainment. Sometimes folks like to place bets on who will win. Chickens aren't much for gambling, but when I heard that Jack Armstong challenged Abraham Lincoln to a wrestling match, I would have bet everything I own (which, unfortunately, isn't a lot) on Jack winning.

The afternoon of the match a bunch of us headed behind the store where a crowd was already gathering. We decided to go partly because we wanted to watch the fight, but also partly because we knew that if there was a crowd there was bound to be snacks. I've been to my share of fights and when folks get excited they let their snacks go flying everywhere, that's when chickens can scoop up some good vittles.

As soon as the fight started I could tell, much to my dismay, that Abraham Lincoln and Jack Armstrong were pretty evenly matched. Lincoln was taller and maybe a bit stronger, but no one could match Armstrong when it came to dirty tricks. I suppose there are rules to wrestling, but from the reaction of the crowd it seems that Armstrong didn't know the rules. He was scratching, and foot stomping, and kicking, but he just wasn't making much progress.

What I saw next was rather shocking. I guess Lincoln had enough of the dirty tricks, so he grabbed Armstrong around the back of the neck, gave him a few shakes, then slammed him onto the ground. What? Was that chowder-headed gollumpus really using my signature move? Instead of being honored, I was outraged, how dare he! He scolded me for doing that to another hen and here he was using it on poor Jack Armstrong! I was going to stomp away in protest but just then someone dropped half a buttered biscuit on the ground, so I had to stay and eat it.

I can't say that Jack Armstrong won the match, nor can I say that Abraham Lincoln won, the truth is, no one won. It ended in a draw. Just when Lincoln was getting the upper hand and ready to send Armstrong home crying, he stopped the match, declared they were evenly matched and victory wasn't possible, then shook hands with his opponent and walked away. Everyone clapped Armstrong on the back and some ran to catch up with Lincoln. I wanted to believe that Lincoln stopped the fight because he feared losing, but when I heard people around me use words like "strength" and "courage" and "respect" for Lincoln, I had to admit that they might be right.

The most surprising thing of all was from that day on, Lincoln and Armstong were the best of friends. Lincoln still didn't drink beer and roll dice, but he and Armstong told jokes and laughed together. They could often be seen around town, sometimes fishing down by the creek, and sometimes just jawing on the porch of the general store.

Over time I started to feel differently about Abraham Lincoln. He was always quick to share his lunch with us when we were scratching around in front of the store, and sometimes he said nice things to us and complimented our chicks when one of us became a mama.

I always wondered why he didn't finish off Jack Armstong in that wrestling match, I think it was because he knew that it was important to show respect by letting Jack keep his dignity. I also got the feeling that even though he was good at fighting, Lincoln didn't much like to fight. I think he believed that fighting should always be a last resort. I also know he believed that it wouldn't help to make the loser of a fight feel like a loser. Maybe he was smarter than I gave him credit for. I don't know what paths he will take in his life, but maybe what he believes will come in handy someday.

Harriet Tubman Leads the Way, Combahee Ferry, South Carolina, 1863

I don't like our rooster. He's mean, bossy, and loud. I suppose he can't help it. Roosters are mean because they can't lay eggs and that makes them feel like they have no purpose. Have you ever noticed that when you see a flock of chickens, most of them are hens and there's only one or two roosters? Chickens are born being able to lay eggs but every now and then one of them is born with something wrong with them and they can't lay eggs, those are roosters. I should feel bad for them, but I don't. Roosters are like misters, I don't like misters either. All the misters I know are mean too. Maybe it's the same way with folks and the misters are the ones born with something wrong with them. Luckily, I have a good missus, so I do my best to avoid all the misters and that rooster.

My missus works as the cook on a rice plantation. Rice is one of the best foods on the planet and since we grow it here, there's plenty of it. Every evening, after the master and his missus have their dinner, we get the plate scrapings which always include rice. Sometimes the rice has gravy on it. I'm not sure what gravy is made of, but it's very tasty. My favorite kind of rice is the rice that my missus has to scrape off the bottom of the pot when she cooks it too long. That kind of rice is crunchy and chickens like crunchy things. One time my missus got distracted while she was tossing us the crunchy rice and when she turned to answer a question she accidentally tossed some rice into the flower bed. When I went to help myself I found out that the rice had landed amongst another of my favorite things- roly polies. Roly polies are also crunchy, so having rice and roly polies together is one of the best meals a chicken could ask for. I hope the master and his missus never find out about the roly polies living in their flower bed because then they would want to have those with rice and gravy for dinner and then there wouldn't be any left for me. I know that's selfish, but that's how I feel about it.

Since I'm my missus's favorite chicken, I like to think I know her best. She and her helper, a younger girl named Rosa, live in a small room just beside the kitchen and I live with the other chickens in a coop nearby. Every morning my missus is the first one up. She has to get up and get the fire going so the master and his wife will have hot water for their baths and for their tea. My missus is the best person in the world. She's so kind to us and she's always humming or singing a song while she works. Rosa says she can't understand why my missus is always singing when they have such a load to bear, but my missus always says that singing gives her the strength so that she *can* bear her load. I don't understand all that, I just know I like to hear her sing.

My missus is a slave, so is Rosa. So is almost everyone who lives here on our rice plantation. I guess that makes me a slave too. I'm not sure what it means to be a slave, but here's what I think it means- It means you have to work very hard and you don't get much rest. It means people can yell at you and hit you anytime they want, and you can't fight back. It means your family and friends can be taken away at any moment and no one will care if that upsets you. But most of all, it means you don't smile hardly at all. My missus hardly ever smiles, but all of that changed the night of the fires.

It started out just like any one of a million ordinary days. I was scratching around by the kitchen door but there was a feeling in the air like something strange was about to happen. Earlier that morning a mister had ridden up fast on his horse. I recognized him since he had been to our place before. Our master ran down the porch steps and met him, they started talking angrily and the master's wife ran down the steps and started to cry when she heard what they were talking about. Remember what I said about misters being mean? Well, my master slapped his missus right in the face, his own missus! He pushed her toward the steps, and she ran back into the house crying and yelling for all the house slaves to come and help her.

The rest of the morning our house slaves helped the master and his missus quickly pack up a wagon. They threw everything they could into that wagon, trunks of clothes, furniture, paintings from the walls, they had so much piled in that wagon I didn't know how the poor horses could even pull it. The missus never stopped crying and the master was yelling mean things at her. Then he tied his saddle horse to the back of the wagon, jumped up on the seat next to his missus and whipped the wagon horses hard so they would go as fast as they could. I saw the plantation overseer ride out on his horse and join them. We all stood still and watched them as long as we could until not even the dust kicked up by the horse's hooves could be seen on the long road that led to whatever else there was in the world.

For the first time in my life I heard nothing. No singing, no shouting, no angry voices, not even any birds. I looked around and saw everyone just standing there, all the field slaves had come in from the fields, the house slaves on the porch, my missus and Rosa standing in the driveway, it's like no one knew what to do next.

We didn't have to wait long. We heard the booming of canons coming from the river and we heard voices. We saw the trees moving, then I realized the trees weren't moving, there were just so many soldiers marching towards us it made it look like the trees were moving. When we saw the soldiers, everyone got scared. We started running around like chickens with our heads cut off since we didn't know where to go. The soldiers were shouting at us that we were free, and we needed to go to the river so we could be taken away to freedom. I had never heard that word before, so I didn't know what freedom was, but my missus sure seemed to know. She and Rosa ran to their room and came back out with everything they owned wrapped up in sacks slung over their shoulders. By now the soldiers were in the house and they started carting away everything my master and his missus didn't put in their wagon. I saw soldiers in the barns leading out the animals and hauling away bags of rice and corn. Then the fires started.

The soldiers set fire to every building on our plantation. I'd seen fire before, but never a fire so big it reached the tops of trees and made smoke so dark it blotted out the sky. I was scared so I started running and squawking at the same time. I glanced back and noticed a soldier chasing me which just made me run faster. Since I was looking behind me and was in a panic, I turned a corner of the house and ran right into my missus who scooped me up quick and held me close to her chest. I could feel her heart beating through her skin and she was making a strange noise, a noise I had never heard her make before. My missus was laughing.

We ran with Rosa and all the other house slaves to the bank of the river where we could see small boats waiting to take us all to a big boat. I was frightened because chickens can't swim and I didn't want to get in that boat. I was also scared because there were so many misters around and I really don't like misters. But as we stepped into the small boat I glanced at the big boat and I saw a missus on the boat. She was giving orders to the soldiers, and they listened to her and did what she said. I had never seen a mister follow a missus's directions before. I found out later that she was Missus Harriet Tubman and not only did she lead folks to freedom, but she worked with the military and was the one to organize the raid that set us free. As we reached the big boat and climbed aboard, she welcomed us. When we passed by her, she reached out and patted my missus on the arm, then she reached over and gave me a few pets on my neck, she said we were both free.

Now I live in a big city called Charleston. My missus has her own little cottage on a pretty, tree-lined street. She goes to work every day and gets money for working. She smiles and sings and plants flowers in boxes in front of her house. In the evenings she has friends come to her cottage and I can hear them laughing and cooking and telling stories through the kitchen's open window.

Before the fires I thought our plantation by the river in South Carolina was the whole world. I didn't know there was anything else. How could I know? But since leaving there I've seen amazing things. I've seen a long line of silver wagons hooked together traveling on tracks faster than a dragonfly right through the city. I've seen buildings and houses built right next to each other in a straight row going down as far as anyone could see. And I've seen missuses with dark skin dressed in nice clothes walking down the street chatting with missuses with white skin and laughing together like that's a perfectly normal thing to do. But the best thing I ever did see was the smile on my missus's face the night we climbed on that boat and she knew she was finally free.

Henry Ford Invents the Horseless Carriage, Detroit, Michigan, 1896

My mister and I have something in common- we both hate horses. He hates them because he says they're messy. I agree, horses are messy. They should be more like chickens; we aren't messy at all. I hate horses because one time a thoughtless horse stepped on my toe and now it's permanently bent! I'm sure he didn't mean to step on my toe, but that was rather careless of him and now I must go through life with a crooked toe. How would he like that? Of course, I know horses don't have toes. Come to think of it, that horse probably stepped on my toe because he was jealous of my toes. My toes were definitely one of my best features, I would often see other hens looking at my toes and I could tell they were envious. But now that I have a crooked toe, no one looks at my feet anymore. That's why I hate horses. I hate horses so much that every time I see a horse I scratch around, acting like I'm minding my own business, then I slowly back up until my rear is just barely touching that horse's leg, then I relieve myself. I have to be sneaky when I'm doing this so I don't get kicked.

My mister hates horses so much that he's busy out in his workshop creating something he calls a "horseless carriage." Once he perfects his invention the world will no longer need horses and then no one will have to worry about their toes. He calls his invention a "quadricycle" and the problem he's tinkering with is that since there won't be any horses involved, something else has to make the carriage go. I thought he should use goats to pull the carriage, I often wonder what the whole purpose of goats is. Pulling a carriage seems like a good job for them, but my mister doesn't want to use any animals at all.

At first, he tried to make his carriage run on steam, but that wasn't the best idea. Then, my mister wanted to make it run using something a friend of his invented called electricity, but that also didn't work. I thought maybe he could use eggs as a power source since everyone knows that eggs are tasty and nutritious. I even hopped up on the quadricycle one Sunday morning while my mister was at church and laid an egg right there on the engine to give him a hint. But I guess he isn't as bright as I thought he was because I don't think he ever tried putting eggs in the engine. Eventually, he did get it to run on something called ethanol, now he drives it all over town, but he still has some tinkering to do because the engine runs too hot.

While my mister spends his time in his workshop with the horseless carriage, I usually head across the street to the potato patch. There are potato patches all over town now. Potato Patch is just another word for a vegetable garden. Times have been tough for the chickens of Detroit because folks don't have a lot of money. When they don't have money to buy food then there aren't any table scraps for the chickens. So, the mayor came up with this idea to turn vacant lots into vegetable gardens so folks can grow their own food and chickens will have table scraps again. Table scraps are the best food a chicken could ever ask for. We get bored if all we get is cracked corn day after day.

I like to head over to the potato patch and help myself to the vegetables. I don't ever really try to get some potatoes because you have to do a lot of digging to reach a potato, and who has time for all that? I generally head straight for the green beans or the cantaloup. It takes some pecking to get to the inside of a cantaloup, but it's worth the effort. Sometimes folks get angry with me and shoo me away from the potato patch garden. I don't know why they do that; don't they know that the whole reason the mayor started this program was because the chickens were suffering? When someone shoos me away I definitely start to fuss just so they'll know that they're wrong to act that way.

One day, while I was helping myself to a big, purple eggplant, which, by the way, isn't made of eggs at all, a missus actually threw a rock at me to get me out of the garden! Getting hit with a rock is very extreme and uncalled for. When that rock hit me, I jumped up off the ground and almost choked on a beak full of eggplant! I took off running, that's how startled I was. If the mayor had been hanging around that day, digging for potatoes, I definitely would have backed my rear up to his shoes because I was thinking that maybe he started this whole potato patch thing just to torture hungry chickens. I was so mad that I sprinted right out of the garden patch and onto the road without looking left and right first. Since I wasn't paying attention I didn't notice my mister was heading straight for me on the horseless carriage! My life flashed before my eyes but at the very last second, my mister swerved to miss me and ran that horseless carriage straight into a ditch filled with water.

My mister was mad. He got out and took his hat off, angrily looking at me and at his poor quadricycle. I could see that one of the tires was bent, a lot like my toe. I decided to keep running full speed for home in case my mister wanted to blame me for what happened. It really was the fault of that missus who threw a rock at me, I wouldn't have had to run out into the street if she had had better manners.

When I reached the gate for our house I looked back and was surprised to see my mister knee deep in water, bending over looking at the engine of his horseless carriage. He didn't look mad, in fact, he looked excited. I found out later that our little accident helped him find a solution to the problem of the engine running too hot. When he ran off the road into the water, it gave him the idea to make water jackets to wrap the fuel tank with to help it cool down. So you see, if it wasn't for me and that eggplant, he would never have gotten the idea to use water to cool down the engine.

My mister's horseless carriage has really taken off, he has an idea to make a whole bunch of them so that even ordinary folks can have one. I'm proud of him, and proud I had a part in it all. Most days, while my mister works on improving his designs. I scratch around in the yard or head over to the potato patch. One time, one of my mister's friends was over for a visit and I heard him ask my mister, "Why is that chicken always crossing the road?" What a dumb question, to get to the other side, of course.

15

Island of Hopes and Dreams, Ellis Island, New York, 1897

"*D* *aj mi trochę ziemniaków.*" That's Polish for, "Give me some of your potato." I've been learning all kinds of languages since I moved here to Ellis Island. I can't actually speak any of the words because chickens can't talk. But I'm learning anyway because when I finally do figure out how to talk, I want to know how to say all the important things.

I didn't set out to live here on Ellis Island, I was supposed to end up in New York. My missus and I traveled all the way from Ireland on a giant boat to get here. It took over two weeks and we had to ride in the bottom of the boat. They called it steerage, that's where all the poor folks had to ride. I didn't need a ticket because my missus hid me inside her overcoat. I'm not a very big chicken, so she was able to hide me well enough to get me on board. Once we were on board no one cared that I was there, everyone was so busy throwing up they hardly even noticed me. Apparently, chickens don't get seasick. Who knew? But it was very boring on the boat. There was nowhere to scratch around and I missed having fresh air. One fellow saw me and asked if I escaped from the kitchen. The kitchen? Why would I be in the kitchen? What a *dummkopf*.

When we finally arrived here on Ellis Island my missus was so weak from throwing up for two weeks she could hardly walk. That's probably why the inspectors took one look at her and chalked her. Getting chalked means you have to stay in the clinic for a while to get checked over by the doctors. They marked my missus's coat with chalk and sent her to the hospital building for an examination. When you get an examination you have to take your clothes off. That's how they found me. That nurse was shocked to see me, I guess she had never seen an honest to goodness Irish chicken before. From the look of amazement on her face I can tell that Irish chickens are much better looking than American chickens.

After a few days they said my missus could go over to New York but that I would have to stay behind. My missus was very *verklempt* to have to leave me, but I think she was anxious to see her family who were waiting for her, so she hustled onto the ferry and off she went. I was sad to see her go, but while she was busy with the doctors one thing I learned about Ellis Island was that there were plenty of people around to pay attention to me and feed me. Lots of folks brought food with them from their countries. I've tasted some of the best treats the world has to offer. Baklava and strudel are my favorites so far.

One of the nurses took a special interest in me and she checks up on me every day. Since there are no predators on Ellis Island, I sleep just about anywhere I want. During the day I wait on the rocks down by the water for the boats to come in. Of course, I have to deal with the seagulls who like to sit on the rocks and blah, blah, blah about everything. Those seagulls sure like to talk. I don't know what they're saying because who speaks seagull? But I can tell whatever it is, it isn't very intelligent conversation. They're basically just waiting for the boats so they can get their greedy beaks on some baklava. They don't even know that the baklava is meant for me, not them. How *estupido* can you be?

Mostly I just wander around amongst the people who are waiting in the long lines to see the immigration officials. A lot of them are scared. They've heard that this place is called "The Island of Tears" because sometimes you go through that two weeks of throwing up in steerage just to get chalked and put right back on a boat for two more weeks of throwing up, and then end up right back where you started from. People don't want that to happen to them. They have dreams that can only come true in America, and they want to stay. I understand that. Maybe my purpose here is to encourage them. I think it makes them happy to see me. I remind them of home. Think about it, wherever you're from in the world there are chickens. We're a very international bird.

So, living here has been a very great experience for me, but I have to admit, when I hear everyone talking about how great America is it makes me want to see for myself. Little did I know that I would soon get my chance.

When the fire first started, I was fast asleep roosting on a beam over the door of the laundry building. Chickens are hard sleepers, I probably would have stayed asleep until my feathers caught on fire if that nice nurse who looked after me hadn't spotted me and grabbed me right off that beam. When I opened my eyes, *oy vey!* The flames were everywhere! People were running and crying and trying to get their luggage out of the building where it was stored. The guards and workers were trying to get everybody to safety. We ran as quickly as we could to the dock where we would be safe. The immigration station burned completely to the ground that night.

No one died in the fire and the officials have vowed to rebuild the station. I'm glad about that. There are so many people who want their chance to come to America. I know no place is perfect, but America is a place where you can dream and not every place in the world is like that. If folks don't have dreams, it's hard to hope that things can get better, and without hope, what is there? America is a land of hopes and dreams and I've learned that those are two of the best words, in any language.

As for me, my nurse friend says she has an aunt who lives in Brooklyn and I can go and live with her. The aunt already has a couple of chickens, so I won't be lonely. When I think about moving away I remember all the words I learned for hope on Ellis Island- *esperanza, hoop, nadzieja, elpizo-* so many words for one important thing. As for me, I can only *hoopas* that they have baklava in Brooklyn.

A Civilian Hero at Gettysburg, Gettysburg, Pennsylvania, 1863

I 'm something my mister calls "skittish." I'm afraid of everyone and everything. The other hens run up fast when it's time for treats and supper scraps, but I just hang back and hope something will fly my way. In the coop I keep to myself, I'm scared of the other hens. I'm not sure why I'm like this, I was born this way. My mister says I'm scared of my own shadow, but he's wrong about that because chickens don't have shadows. I'm pretty sure some of the hens think I should change and become more friendly, but since being skittish saved my life at the Battle of Gettysburg, maybe change is overrated.

All the folks in our town say my mister is old and crazy. They think he's old because he's grumpy, and they think he's crazy because he tried to volunteer to fight in the war even though folks of his age aren't good fighters. When he was told he was too old, he got mad and even more cantankerous than usual.

Most folks in our neighborhood don't like my mister all that much, but that's because they don't know his good side. My mister knows

I don't often get the best table scraps because I'm too timid to get in there and wrestle for them with the other hens, so sometimes he picks out a piece of boiled green bean, or a crust of a piece of bread, and throws it in my direction when I'm far enough away to be the only hen who can get it. So, you see, my mister isn't all bad.

One day, the rebels began to fight close by and some of them even wandered into town and took over. Since my mister was the town constable, he started harassing them and tried to kick them out of town. Those soldiers didn't like that, so they ended up arresting him and putting him in our own town jail. He sure made a fuss about that, we could hear him hollering all the way at our house! But then the Union soldiers began to show up and drive the Confederates out of town. Then my mister got out of jail and went looking for stragglers to capture.

On the day the battle started my mister was not about to be left behind. I'll never forget how he looked when he walked down the porch steps dressed in his overcoat and top hat, carrying an old flintlock rifle. My missus was yelling at him, calling him an "old fool" for going to fight at his age. But for a man who always had a scowl on his face, I thought he had never looked happier. I hoped with all my heart that he would come back.

As my mister walked down the street, I heard neighbors fussing at him and telling him to go home before he got his head shot off. Though I'm a skittish hen, I'm also a very curious hen and since my mister is the only one who ever understood me, I decided to follow behind him as long as I could and try to keep him safe.

Since my mister is old, I didn't have to walk very fast to keep up with him. That's good because I'd never been so far away from

21

home before. I decided to take the opportunity to taste some of the neighborhood bugs in case there were some that we didn't have in our own backyard. I thought I saw a beetle that looked more exotic than any I had ever seen, but when I got closer, I saw it just had a mushy leaf stuck to its back. I ate it anyway; the mushy leaf was kind of like gravy.

Eventually my mister came upon a couple of soldiers stumbling into town because they were wounded. One of them was bleeding from his belly and the other one was bleeding from his head. My mister yelled at them and said some unpleasant words that I know better than to repeat. He told them that a little blood shouldn't keep them from fighting the rebels and he called them cowards for running away from the fight. I had to agree with my mister on that one. One time I got one of my toenails caught on an old board and it tore my nail clean off. Did I let that stop me? Of course not! I kept scratching around and walking on my foot even though I was in pain. These two so-called soldiers didn't even have wounds on their feet like I did, and they were acting like they couldn't fight any more? Give me a break! Getting shot in the stomach or the head is nothing compared to having your toenail ripped clean off. Well, while my mister was yelling at them the one with the bullet in his stomach collapsed right there on the street, so my mister traded rifles with him and loaded his pockets with ammunition. I was glad to see that my mister had a better rifle now, I've seen him shoot at wild hogs from the porch steps with that flintlock rifle and let's just say we never got a lot of table scraps that included ham and bacon.

We kept going and I took care to keep back and out of the way, running from one porch to the next. That got harder when we got to the open ground near the McPherson Woods. That's where my mister met up with some officers and he asked if he could fight with them. While they were chatting, I sprinted into the woods and found an old hollow log to hide in. My plan was to stay there until everyone left and then head back to the neighborhood. The only problem was that in no time at all there were soldiers everywhere and they were all shooting at each other! Well, I didn't want to get shot so I hunkered down in that old log and waited it out. I might have starved to death if not for the termites. I do like a tasty termite and there were plenty of them. So, as the battle raged all around me, I had my snacks and waited for it to be over.

Every now and then I could hear the unmistakable sound of my mister hollering at this and that. I was glad to hear his voice because it made me feel less alone. I thought there might be room in the log for him to squeeze in if he wanted a little rest, but then I thought he might be hungry, and I didn't want to share my termites. Besides, I didn't quite know how to suggest it. Eventually, things got quiet in the woods, and I figured it was as good a time as any to get some sleep.

I must have slept all night because I was awakened the next morning by the sound of my mister talking to himself. I looked through a crack in the log and saw my mister acting strangely. I saw him hide his rifle in the bushes and then dig a hole. At first I thought he was digging a hole so he could take a dust bath. Dust baths can be very relaxing after a hard day. But instead of hopping in that hole he emptied his pockets of all his ammunition and buried it. I could soon see why, there were some soldiers heading for him and they had their rifles pointed at him! I thought the end had surely come for my mister and that would be a problem because without him I wouldn't know how to get home. Well, my mister started telling those soldiers that he hadn't been in the battle himself, but that he was cutting through the field to go and find a doctor because his missus was weak and sick. This didn't make sense to me because from the way the missus was hollering at my mister yesterday, she was anything but weak and sick. I guessed my mister was telling a tale so those soldiers wouldn't shoot him in the foot and make him lose his toenail. Those soldiers got tired of listening to him go on and on (my mister is quite a talker) so they picked him up and took him away.

Now all was quiet in the woods. I could still hear shots and cannons firing in the distance, so I knew the battle was still going. But since I didn't know the way home, I wasn't quite sure what to do. I knew I would run out of termites soon, but it was starting to get dark and I'm afraid of the dark. I decided to sleep in the log one more night then head for town in the morning.

The next morning I woke up bright and early. I could see flashes of light on Seminary Hill, so I knew the battle was still on, but I was out of termites and needed to find my way home. I sprinted out of that log and headed towards town. Once I got there, I wandered around, trying to stay out of sight. I walked around all day until I was so tired that I could hardly go on. I happened upon a caterpillar just in the nick of time since I was starting to faint from hunger. As I sat in a mulberry bush eating my caterpillar, trying not to despair, I suddenly heard a familiar holler. It was my mister! He seemed to be yelling at a doctor for charging too much. I rushed out of the bushes and headed toward the sound. Three houses down I saw my own house and saw the doctor leaping into his carriage, whipping his horses into a gallop, desperate to get away from our house, my mister cursing him as he went. I was finally home!

My mister recovered from his injuries even though some neighbors thought he got what he deserved for being an old fool. But my mister got the last laugh because some months later the town dedicated a cemetery to the soldiers who died and none other than Abraham Lincoln came to speak. As it turns out, the president requested specifically to chat with my mister and called him a hero. I'll never forget the look on my missus's face when President Abraham Lincoln knocked on the door!

I'm still skittish and my mister is still grumpy, but maybe it's OK to not be who everyone says we ought to be. At least I think it is.

Surrender at Appomattox Court House, Appomattox Court House, Virginia, 1865

I almost became a Civil War souvenir not once but twice! This is how it happened...

When I was a young pullet, I lived with my mister and missus in Manassas. We lived in a peaceful farmhouse, at least it was peaceful until a mister named General Beauregard came to stay. Of course, we all knew there we were on the verge of war, we just didn't know the war was coming to our own backyard.

One morning General Beauregard was in the dining room having his breakfast. He sure loved breakfast. He always had scrambled eggs, bacon, and a big glass of milk. I was proud that my farm friends and I were able to provide breakfast for the General. The eggs came from me, the milk came from Hilda, our milk cow, and the bacon came from the pig. I'm not sure about that pig's name, but it doesn't matter now since I haven't seen that pig in a while. Come to think of it, that pig disappeared right around the time the General came to stay with us.

During breakfast we heard this horrible sound, as it turns out, it was a cannonball fired at our house! It landed right down in the kitchen fireplace. I guess that means no more scrambled eggs for the General.

That cannonball was the first of many, in fact, the battle was fought right in our backyard! Usually, I'm pretty brave about things but when the cannonballs started flying and the misters came sprinting through the front yard with their muskets, I ran under the porch. All afternoon I hid under the porch while the fighting raged on. I began to wonder if I would starve to death under that porch, but luckily I was able to secure a couple of large spiders. Normally I don't eat spiders because there isn't much to them once you deal with all those legs, but desperate times call for desperate measures.

As evening came and the battle died down, I decided to scoot out from under the porch and head for the coop. Hiding all day was tiring. As I crossed the yard I was happy to see my mister and missus had gotten through the battle just fine. There was no sign of that General Beauregard, I thought that was for the best since he was such a big egg eater, and I wasn't in the mood to lay eggs. As I walked I noticed some soldiers milling about, I thought they were stragglers who were late catching up with their soldier friends, but then I noticed that one of them was carrying a rake from the barn and another one had pried off the handle from the well. I thought those were odd things to be stealing but then I heard an empty handed one say, "Look at that chicken! I'm sure someone would pay a lot of money for a chicken who survived the first big battle of the war!" Then he lunged at me!

It's a good thing I had eaten those spiders earlier in the day because they gave me the energy to outrun him. Nutrition is important. I was able to make it to the elm tree and with a mighty jump and flap of my wings I flew to the lowest branch and then kept hopping as far up into the branches as I could get. That soldier tried to climb up after me, but he was too fat and the branch he was holding on to broke and then he fell and split the seam of his pants wide open. I was embarrassed for him. That's why I don't wear pants, too many things can go wrong.

After those soldiers left, things calmed down at our farm. My mister said the war would only last a few months; I was glad for that. I didn't want to have to hide under the porch again and have nothing to eat but spiders.

After a year or two my mister realized that it had been longer than a few months and the war was still going. My missus talked him into leaving Manassas because she was scared of all the Yankees wandering around all over the place, so we packed up everything and moved to a dusty town called Appomattox Court House. It was far enough away that we wouldn't have to worry about the war being fought in our yard again. That's a good thing because I haven't figured out how to get under the porch at this new house.

We spent several peaceful years in our new home until off in the distance we heard a familiar sound, cannonballs- again. I guess my mister and missus were pretty popular because those soldiers followed us out to Appomattox Court House and started fighting down by the creek. Since I couldn't get under the porch and we didn't have any high trees to fly up into, I decided to hide in the smokehouse. That was an eye-opener. Let's just say that I know where bacon comes from now.

I hid all morning with the bacon but the battle never came to our yard. What did come to our yard was a messenger. He knocked on my mister's door and asked if some soldiers could meet inside my mister's house and talk about how the war was going. My mister said no problem, and before I could swallow a spider (I've grown to rather enjoy them) our yard was full of important looking soldiers on horses. I recognized two of them from seeing their pictures in the newspapers my mister would leave out under the shade tree by the chair where he takes his afternoon naps. Their names were General Lee and General Grant. Great, more generals.

I don't know what exactly happened in my mister's parlor but whatever it was ended the war. When they all came out of the house, I saw a lot of hand shaking and then the generals got up on their horses and trotted away in different directions. That's when the souvenir collecting began again. Soldiers started dragging furniture out of my mister's house because they wanted a souvenir of the place where the war ended. Well, I'd been through that before and since I didn't want to be a souvenir chicken I stayed in the smokehouse with the bacon. By the way, bacon- YUM!

Those soldier souvenir hunters took everything but the kitchen sink and left my mister and missus with no table to have their breakfast on. That's good because no one had time to lay any eggs and even though I knew we had bacon, I kind of wanted to keep all that bacon to myself because bacon is way better than spiders. My mister didn't seem too bothered about losing his furniture, he mostly just seemed happy the war was finally over. I heard him chuckle and say, "The war began in my front yard and ended in my front parlor." I guess my mister could still find a reason to laugh after all he'd been through. It just goes to show you that even if trouble seems to follow you everywhere you go, that doesn't mean you have to let it get you down.

Hot Air Balloons Join the Battle, Gaines Mill, Virginia, 1862

My best friend is a pig named Clara. I don't think Clara knows she's my best friend, but I intend to make sure she realizes it soon. The reason I want her to be my friend is that she has something I need, and without it, I'll never make my dream come true.

My dream is to fly. I was born to fly. Of course chickens can fly a little bit. We can fly up onto a low tree branch, but that's about it. We can't fly like real birds. How can I be content scratching around on the ground with the poultry when I was born to soar through the air like an eagle?

When I was a chick I used to hop up on my mother's back and sit up there, looking down at my brothers and sisters and enjoying the view. Now that I'm older I do my best to sleep at the top of the roost, which is tricky, due to the pecking order. Technically, I'm too young to have earned a spot at the top, but I'm smarter than everyone else. I wait until it's almost completely dark and the old hens have dozed off, then I stealthily hop rung by rung, to the top of the roost. Imagine how shocked the old girls are in the morning when they wake up and see me nestled in between them snoozing with my head tucked into my neighbor's feathers to stay warm.

When I'm outside I always fly up into a tree and hop from branch to branch. I like to get as high up as I can so that I can study the birds and learn their ways, but also because there are tasty bugs high up in the trees that the chickens on the ground have only ever dreamed of. It was while I was up in a tree that I got the idea about Clara the pig.

It was a warm June day and I had spent the morning hopping from branch to branch in the tallest walnut tree on the farm. From high on my perch, I could see my lowly chicken friends scratching around in the dirt below me. What a sad existence they had! They dreamed of nothing more than grub worms and larvae- I dreamed of the sky, the clouds, the heavens above! Just as I was thinking these glorious thoughts a cannonball whizzed to the left of me and took out a huge branch of the tree. It surprised me so much I decided to stop daydreaming and pay attention to what was going on around me. From my perch I noticed there was a lot of commotion on our farm. Chickens were running everywhere, then misters with guns began running all over the place. We'd heard all this talk about a war going on, but it had never been going on in our own backyard before. War is very noisy. While all this was going on below, I lifted my eyes to the skies and saw a very unusual thing. I saw a mister sitting in a basket high up in the air. He seemed to be looking down, trying to find something on the ground below, probably caterpillars. This time of the year there are a lot of caterpillars and they sure are a good meal. But then I noticed that every now and then he would drop something out of the basket and the misters down below him would catch it and run away excitedly with it. I think he was sending them messages about what he was seeing from up there. Then I saw another mister farther away rising into the air in the same sort of contraption! He sure was a brave one, as that basket was rising some of the misters on the ground were shooting at it. What was going on? I was instantly jealous! I'd never seen a mister fly before, misters don't even have wings! I knew there must be a trick to it and if a mister could figure it out, surely, I could too. Chickens are way smarter than people, and the proof of that was right below me. When was the last time you saw chickens chasing each other around with guns?

The baskets they were sitting in were attached to giant eggs. Well, they looked like eggs, but I wasn't sure they actually were eggs. I once laid an egg on a shelf in the barn and it rolled right off and smashed all over the floor, it didn't hang in the air like they did. I've only ever seen one other thing that looked like them and could do what those giant eggs were doing- a pig bladder.

I've had some experience with pig bladders since every year at hog butchering time (that's the time of the year when pigs give the misters their bladders) my mister would wash off the bladder, blow some air into it, tie it off, then give it to children to play with. They would have a great time with that pig bladder. They would kick it around the yard, toss it to each other, and throw it in the air. I remembered that a pig bladder seemed to suspend itself in the air a bit longer than if it had been something solid. But it wasn't until I saw those misters in the baskets suspended in the air by a giant pig bladder that I realized if I wanted to fly like I was meant to, I needed to get myself a pig bladder. That's when I thought of Clara.

Clara is the biggest pig on our farm, and since I'm smaller than a mister, I think her bladder will do just fine. For some reason, she doesn't seem to want to part with it. After the battle I spent a lot of time hanging around her. I noticed that she seemed to get fatter every day. Once I jumped on to her back and rode around up there half the afternoon, but then I got bored and flew down. Clara didn't seem to have any other friends so you would think after a few days of me hanging around she would have been grateful enough for my friendship to give me her bladder, but she was a stubborn pig. I became obsessed with my dream to fly and decided to just steal her bladder if I had to. I started attacking her middle, I figured she was probably hiding her bladder in there since it was her biggest part. I would rush at her and peck her as hard as I could. Naturally, she didn't much like that and took to turning on me and trying to grab me. I knew enough about pigs to realize that pigs sometimes get a hankering for a chicken dinner, so after a few days of this behavior I decided to end my friendship with Clara. A day or two later Clara gave birth to fourteen piglets. She was a lot skinnier after that.

The war has moved on now and I haven't seen any more misters in baskets. After my idea failed, I got depressed. I moped around and tried to be content with a life on the ground. My only happiness was when I could muster the energy to hop up into my secret hideaway in the walnut tree. One afternoon I was sulking up amongst the branches watching my mister and his son as they walked out into the field below with their rifles. While I was sitting up there desolate and alone, I was joined by a small flock of doves. Such sweet birds, they make such soft, lovely noises. They fly from tree to tree and soar into the air with such majesty, they don't even know how lucky they are.

Just then that pretty little flock of doves lifted their delicate wings and took off into the bright, clear air. They didn't last long. My mister and his son lifted their rifles and shot every one of those doves out of the sky. That was an unexpected turn of events.

Ever since that day I have a great time scratching around with my colleagues on the beautiful earth God created. I don't hop around in the walnut tree anymore, and I don't spend time remembering those misters in their flying baskets. Flying is a noble thing, but it has its hazards. I've decided to be content with who I am instead of always wishing to be somebody I'm not.

Carpetbagger Chickens, Atlanta, Georgia, 1867

When I finally met the Yankees who moved in next door, I was a tad bit disappointed. My missus said they were horrible and selfish and were only here to take advantage of us Southerners. She said they were Carpetbaggers, which is even worse than being a Scalawag, whatever that is. I expected them to be monsters, but they weren't. They seemed normal, even nice. One of them chased a grasshopper until it crossed over into our yard then stopped so I could snatch it for myself. I thought that was only right, after all, it did come into my yard.

The Yankees moved into the house next door because after the war was over, the Dolans, who lived there for generations, never came back. I don't know what all happened during the war since I wasn't hatched yet, but my missus says that Atlanta was taken over by the Yankees and they even burned some of our great city down. Folks were so scared that they left their homes and went to live out in the country. I guess some of them just decided to stay in the country and not come back, that's why carpetbaggers can live in their houses now.

While we're out scratching around in the yard my missus and her daughter do the laundry and talk. They don't like our carpetbagger neighbors because they have more money than we do. They're fixing up the old Dolan house and since my missus says she doesn't even have enough money for hair pins, she can't fix up our place. Chickens don't wear hairpins. It's not just the money that bothers my missus, she says the Yankees have strange ways. Her daughter tells her she's just jealous of the Yankees, that's why she thinks they're strange. But my missus disagreed. I think she's just determined to hate those Yankees. Yesterday afternoon the Yankee missus brought a plate of cookies over for my missus. My missus said, "No thank you," and turned around and walked back in the house. I thought she should have at least accepted the cookies and given them to us if she didn't want them. Chickens like cookies and we don't care if a Yankee baked them.

Since I wasn't sure what my missus meant about Yankees having strange ways, I decided to investigate for myself. Our yards don't have fences, just a hedge with gaps in it, so if I find a small gap in the hedges, I can see what's going on with our neighbors. Since most of them have red feathers, and I have red feathers too, I decided no one would notice if I wandered over there and had a look around, so that's what I did. The first thing I noticed was that they had a pan full of grain so they could all have as much cracked corn as they wanted all day long. We just get a handful scattered on the grass every morning. I started to understand what my missus meant about being jealous, I sure would like to have as much corn as I could eat. But then maybe our yard would get overrun with beetles because I wouldn't be hunting them down and eating them every day because I would be too full of corn to get around quickly. Maybe those Yankees don't know how important it is to have their chickens eat beetles. Other than the pan of corn, everything else seemed normal in their yard, so I got bored and went home.

Since it was a hot afternoon, I decided to take a dust bath in the shade of the hedges, that way I could keep my eyes on the neighbors and see if they were up to anything. It's a good thing I did because if I hadn't decided on that dust bath in the hedges, I would have missed out on seeing the most shocking thing I have ever seen!

Late in the afternoon the Yankee missus came out her back door carrying what I thought was a baby. She sat down on a bench under a shade tree and started to unwrap a white cloth that was around that baby's bottom. My missus's daughter has a baby, so I know all about that white cloth, it's best to steer clear of it if you ever see it laying around. Anyways, she was talking sweetly to the baby, but I was only half paying attention because the sun was hot and I was getting sleepy. Besides, I've seen my share of babies in my life and they're nothing special to look at. As I was dozing off, I noticed something peculiar. It took my brain a few moments to register that what I was seeing wasn't a baby, could it be? Heavens to Betsy! It was a chicken! She unwrapped that chicken and put it on the lawn so it could scratch around, then she took a book out of her pocket and started to read there in the shade. Were my eyes deceiving me or did I just see something I've always heard about, but never believed to be true?

I continued to stare at them for I don't know how long, just wanting to confirm my suspicions. It must have been close to an hour before the sun shifted and the missus started to get warm. That's when she took a folded up white cloth out of her other pocket, picked up the chicken, and proceeded to wrap its bottom in that white cloth with space for the legs to poke through. She pinned the cloth together on top with a giant pin, picked that chicken up, and walked with it straight back into the house. It was true, the Yankees next door had an honest to goodness house chicken.

All my life I had heard rumors of chickens that live in the house with the misters and missuses, but I had never believed it was true. I don't think anyone else in our coop believed it either. But now I had proof. That night, as I tried to sleep, I thought of that house chicken sleeping in a bed with her missus, dreaming of whatever Yankees dream of at night. I wondered if that chicken ate cookies all day and had a special tub for dustbathing in the house. I wondered what it would be like to eat all the good food you wanted and live inside a pleasant house with no other chickens to bother you. And as I slept, a small flicker of jealousy grew, and I woke up the next morning with an ugly heart.

From that morning on my jealousy consumed me. If any of the Yankee chickens even got close to the hedges I ran out and attacked them. I snuck over to their side and gorged on their corn. Then, I scratched the Yankee missus's flower beds all to pieces. I wandered out to the front of our houses and snuck over to their porch and relieved myself on their freshly painted steps. I was gratified when that evening I saw the Yankee mister come home from work and slip on the steps on the present I left for him. It got to the point where all I could think about was those Yankees and how they had come here with their money and their house chicken, flaunting in our faces all that we didn't have.

After a few days of my behavior, I noticed I wasn't even laying eggs any more. That's what happens when you get so consumed with hate, you can't even accomplish the most important things in life. I plopped down under the shade of the hedges, but even a dust bath couldn't make me feel better. I watched glumly as the Yankee missus came out of her house with that diaper wearing chicken and set it down in the grass in front of the bench. I watched, hating that chicken even though it had never done anything to me. As I watched, I saw something peculiar, something I had somehow not noticed before. That chicken was limping, not just a slight limp, but a limp so great it could hardly walk. I stood up so I could see better and that's when I saw that the toes on one of its feet were completely curled under, that chicken couldn't hardly walk in that condition, and it sure couldn't scratch.

As I sat back down I used my feet to kick some dust over me. As the cool dust settled on my skin and cleaned me off I thought of what it would be like if I couldn't take a dust bath. Worse, what if I could never scratch around in the dew-covered grass for an earthworm? I don't even know if life would be worth living without worms, that's how good they are. As I glanced at that chicken again, standing lopsided in the grass, pecking at what it could reach from where it stood, my heart began to soften. The chicken world is not one where we help each other out and I had no doubt that the only reason that chicken was even still alive is because that missus cared for it and let it sleep in the house where it would be safe.

I decided that it was time to change my heart and choose to let the jealousy fall away. Did those Yankees have more money than us? Yes. Did they have strange ways? Yes. But anyone who could care for a lame chicken and save its life couldn't be as bad as I had imagined. Maybe it was time for the war to be over. Maybe it was time to try and understand each other and help each other become the best that we can be. I would probably never be a house chicken, but I could be the best regular chicken that I could be, and that's just what I decided to do.

Sallie, the War Hero, Annapolis, Maryland, 1861

My mister says that girls are nothing but trouble. That's why I wasn't too excited when Sallie arrived at our camp. She came in with a group of soldiers called the 11th Pennsylvania Infantry and let me tell you, those soldiers sure thought Sallie was something special. I think Sallie thought she was special too, she had big brown eyes, shiny hair, and a cute, little nose. I didn't see what all the fuss was about. From what I could see, she was just your average, everyday dog.

I live with about thirty other hens out behind the mess hall. Our mister's name is Cook and he's in charge of making huge meals for the soldiers who are garrisoned here. Cook expects us to lay an egg a day. He says there's a war on and we must do our part. I'm no shirker and I intend to do my part, maybe even lay two eggs a day, if I can.

Cook is very good to us. He calls us his "little soldiers" and treats us well. He makes all the men scrape their supper leftovers into a bucket so he can save it for us. I love bucket time, you never know what you're going to get. But I don't just love Cook for the food he gives us; I love him for his kindness. Sometimes Cook will bring a stool out under a shade tree, then he lugs a giant sack of potatoes and an empty pot out there so he can peel potatoes and enjoy the breeze at the same time. I like to jump up on his lap while he's peeling and listen to him tell stories about the place where he grew up. I don't understand most of what he's saying, chickens only know a few words, but I like to listen to his voice while he's talking, it puts me to sleep. Sometimes he carves out a little piece of potato for me to have for a snack, but I never eat the potato peels. No self-respecting chicken ever eats potato peels. So, you can see why I was so angry when Sallie turned Cook against me.

Chickens and dogs are not known for their companionship. Dogs can be rough with chickens, even if they don't mean to be. I once heard a story about a flock of chickens minding their own business in their own yard, when a dog decided to come over to play. Well, he played with those chickens until they were all dead! He didn't eat them and wasn't doing it out of meanness, he was just having a good time and didn't stop to consider that he was a lot stronger than them. When he grabbed them and shook them in his mouth, it was just too much for them to handle. So, when Sallie showed up here at our post, I was determined not to let her play with any of us.

Sallie wasn't the first pet to come riding into camp, regiments of soldiers were always hauling along a troop mascot or two. I've seen cats, goats, and even a pet pig wandering around amongst the tents taking handouts from the soldiers and sleeping on blankets next to them. But this Sallie was different. She didn't just hang around the tents, she was the first to arrive at roll call. She jumped around and

43

barked while the men performed drills. She loved to march in front, next to the commanding officer's horse, whenever they marched to their assignments. It's almost like she thought she was a soldier. I must admit, I did admire her a bit for that. I wish I could be a soldier, but my knees don't bend in the right way for marching.

All my admiration flew the coop, though, on the afternoon Sallie got bored and decided to pay us a visit. Like I said, dogs are frisky and like to chase chickens, and that's just what Sallie did. We were out taking our dust baths behind the mess hall when a blur of brown fur rushed upon us, slinging slobber from her tongue as she barked and ran towards us from around the corner. We panicked and started running in every direction. I was so scared that I cut to the left suddenly and ran between the legs of a rickety bench that was holding the giant pot of beans that Cook had left out to soak. That dumb dog was chasing me so fast that though she tried to stop, she skidded straight into that bench and dumped that pot of beans all over the dirt. Over a bushel of wet beans cascaded like a river making a muddy mess right under the clothesline. Even that didn't stop Sallie, she continued to chase me and because I was so scared I flapped my wings and tried to fly fast away from her. I ended up flying straight into an apron that was hanging from the clothesline. Because I got tangled up in the apron, that slowed me down and Sallie was able to try to leap up to grab me, but she ended up missing and grabbed the apron instead. That dog hauled the whole clothesline down! Dozens of tablecloths, dish rags, aprons, towels, and even Cook's pants joined the beans in the muddy river flowing through our yard.

All that commotion got Cook's attention and he came running out of the kitchen yelling at us at the top of his voice. By now I was untangled from the apron and was slogging through the mud on my way to a safer part of the yard. I was glad Cook was there because he could deal with that crazy dog, but to my shock, Cook hurled a ladle straight at me! That scared me more than the dog because it was so unexpected. I didn't understand why he was mad at me, why wasn't he angry at Sallie? But by glancing around I knew why- Sallie was gone. She must have high tailed it out of there as soon as she heard Cook's voice. Cook thought it was the chickens who caused all the fuss!

That was the start of a dark time for me. Cook was my best friend and now he was so mad at us that he didn't peel potatoes in the yard anymore. He still brought us a bucket of scraps each evening, but he didn't sing his "Chickie, Chickie" song when he dumped the scraps in the dirt. I was devastated.

A few days later I was still so depressed that I didn't notice when a hen let out an alarm squawk and started running to the safety of the coop. The other hens followed close behind her but lost in my own sad memories of afternoons under the shade tree with Cook and the potatoes, I didn't notice the bobcat until it was almost upon me. It would have been a quick death for me, probably instant since a bobcat always goes straight for the throat. But just as I turned and saw the blur of fur about to pounce, from the corner of my eye I saw that familiar silky, shiny hair and I knew Sallie had come to rescue me. The bobcat screeched and Sallie growled as they rolled on the ground as one. The fight seemed to go on forever, but it couldn't have been more than a few seconds before the bobcat took off running, never to be seen again. Sallie was left with a cut over her eye, I watched as she tilted her head down and rubbed the blood on her leg. Then she looked at me with those big brown eyes, slobber dripping from her smiling mouth. She turned and trotted out of the yard and back to her regiment, ready to fight another day.

It's been several years since the day Sallie saved my life. I'm old now and this war is finally coming to an end. Cook's hair is getting gray, I notice it when I sit on his lap on sunny afternoons as we peel potatoes in the yard. I've kept up with news of my friend Sallie, she's become quite a soldier over the years. The whole camp buzzed with the story of Sallie at the Battle of Gettysburg. She stayed by the side of her fallen comrades on the battlefield for three days, refusing to leave them. We were proud to hear that, proud that she had been one of our own.

I was sitting with Cook when the news came of her death. She was shot in battle at a place called Hatcher's Run. Her fellow soldiers buried her there on the battlefield. They wept as they dug, the enemy firing at them as tears dropped on their shovels. But not even bullets could keep them from digging the grave that would forever be her resting place. Chickens can't cry, but if we could, I would have cried then for the bravest dog I ever knew- my friend, Sallie.

Sailing to Freedom, Charleston, South Carolina, 1862

L ots of folks say that roosters are supposed to be mean, and tough, and grumpy, but I can't help it if my favorite thing to do is jump up on my little missus's lap and get some cuddles. I know I should be training to be a leader of the flock and learn from my elders, but I think, when the time comes, I'll be as tough as anyone when I need to be. Why can't I fight off a hawk to save a hen, then strut over and get some hugs? Maybe I can be what I want to be, not what others expect me to be.

I think I like snuggles so much because of the little missus who raised me. My own mother hatched me and then decided she would rather catch grasshoppers than be tied down with a chick to raise. The little missus heard me putting up a fuss all by myself in a corner of the coop and scooped me up and took me home to sleep in a box next to her pallet on the floor.

The little missus and her ma live in a shack behind the big house. They work in the house from the time the sun comes up until it's so dark you can't see your feathers right in front of your face. The little missus scrubs the floors and does the laundry and takes care of all the animals, her ma runs the kitchen and makes the beds and sews the master's breeches. When I was little, and still slept in the shack with them, I used to hear ma tell little missus stories about a faraway place they would go to someday. She called the place Freedom. Apparently, in Freedom, the little missus and her ma won't have to work so hard. They'll get to eat good food and wear nice clothes. Maybe Freedom is a place where you get all the good things that you want. If that's the case, for me, Freedom will have more caterpillars than I can eat, and plenty of worms, and of course, lots of cuddles and hugs. I wonder how far away Freedom is from Charleston?

One night, when I was fast asleep on the roost with the other chickens, the little missus slipped into the coop and scooped me up. I didn't fuss because I knew she meant me no harm, also because I was pretty tired. She slipped me down inside her shirt, since I was only a little more than four months old, I fit just fine and when she put her shawl on over us, no one even knew I was there. She whispered to me "We goin' to Freedom!" I closed my eyes and dozed off dreaming of all the good things that waited for me in Freedom- mostly caterpillars and worms.

When I woke up, I could smell the ocean and there was a crowd of people with us, they seemed pretty nervous. Somehow, I knew I needed to keep quiet. I tried to go back to sleep but some of the folks were crying and talking about what would happen if we got caught. I was starting to think that maybe this trip to Freedom wasn't such a good idea when suddenly I felt the little missus lift her arms and we were swung through the air landing on the deck of a boat.

Being from a port city I knew what a boat was, I also knew that boats went in the water and since I wasn't a duck, I didn't think being in the water was the best place for me. But I trusted my little missus and kept my beak shut. It took only a few minutes for us to climb down some steps and everything got even darker than it was outside. Once my eyes adjusted to the dim light, I could peek out from between the buttons of her shirt and see that we were in the hold of a ship. There were some guns down there, and cannons. The little missus's ma was with us, and so were a lot of other misters and missuses I had never seen before. I was so curious I couldn't help but stretch my neck out even more to have a better look around, and that's when someone saw me.

"Look there, in her shirt, is that a chicken?"

"We caint have a chicken onboard, it's liable to make noise and give us away!"

"Hand it over to me, I cain wring its neck real quiet like."

That last voice was low with a hard edge to it. I don't know what the word "wring" means, but it sure doesn't rhyme with "snuggle," "cuddle," and "hugs."

Then another voice spoke up, "Let's toss it overboard quick."

"No, if someone sees us toss it, they'll know we up to something."

By this time, I was sitting on my little missus's lap. I tried to press myself even closer to her because I was starting to get nervous. Just then, a little boy who was sitting in his mother's arms started to whimper. He was scared and started to cry, pretty soon he was outright wailing. Now everyone forgot about me and started to worry about what they were going to do to keep him quiet. I noticed no one suggested tossing him overboard.

While everyone was trying to get that child to calm down, out of the corner of my eye I saw something crawling on the floor that could only be one thing- breakfast. It was a cockroach, a big one with a shiny back. I couldn't help myself; I leaped off the little missus's lap and started to chase it. I stretched out my neck and got my head low and ran as fast as I could, but that roach was speedy. It was dark, and my head was so low that I didn't see the cannon directly ahead of me and I ran right smack into it and ended up flying backwards to land on my rump hard. That's when I heard it, a very soft giggle. As I was shaking my head and trying to get my senses back, I noticed that everyone was silently watching me and that little boy had stopped his fussing and was laughing at my misfortune. I should have been offended at that, but since the cockroach was back on the move the chase was back on and this time, I caught it. It tasted like Freedom.

That's when we heard the ship's whistle blow, I almost jumped out of my feathers it was so loud! I heard someone whisper that it meant we were passing by Fort Johnson. My little missus scurried over and picked me up and crawled up the stairs with me. We kept low so no one could see us, but from the top stair we could peek out and I saw a mister named Robert Smalls. He was standing there all official like, wearing a captain's hat and steering the boat. Robert Smalls was a slave and it had been his idea to steal this ship and sail us all to Freedom. As we approached Fort Sumter he flashed the Navy signal to the watchers and kept going. He didn't flinch, and he didn't seem nervous or scared as he stood there pretending to be the captain. I knew what I was watching right in front of me was the strongest, bravest rooster I had ever seen. I also knew that he could probably have gotten to Freedom a lot easier without all of us in tow, that meant he had a soft side and might be fond of a snuggle or two as well.

Once we passed Fort Sumter, we could see off in the distance boats that flew a different flag, I thought they must be the Yankees I had heard so much about. There was a commotion behind us below deck, I knew they were peering out the portholes and saw what we saw- a ship up ahead had aimed its big gun straight at us. That's when a missus brushed past and handed a white bed sheet to one of Robert Small's helpers. Some of the misters on deck quickly lowered the rebel flag and replaced it with the white sheet and then hoisted it up. I was worried that the Yankees wouldn't see it in time and I would never make it to Freedom. But that ship never fired and Mister Robert Smalls never wavered. When we could see the misters on that Yankee boat waving at us my little missus and I were almost trampled by all the folks running up the stairs. We stood up and joined them on deck, laughing and dancing and singing. As we got close enough to be heard by the men on the other boats, Mister Robert Smalls shouted out to the Yankee captain, "Good Morning sir, I've brought you some of the old United States guns, sir!" That captain sure looked shocked to see all of us. Some of them pointed at me and I know they were pointing because they had never seen such a brave rooster before.

As we sailed past them I knew we had reached the place little missus had whispered to me about. I didn't see any worms or slugs, so I knew Freedom was different than what I had expected it to be. But as my little missus hugged me and jumped up and down and laughed and sang, I knew that Freedom was more than a place, it was a way of life. As we sailed on and the sun rose over the water, for the first time in my life- I crowed.

America's Pastime, Elysian Fields, Hoboken, New Jersey, 1846

Something very embarrassing and a little bit painful happened to me today. I suppose it's my fault. I know I'm not supposed to go off wandering by myself, but the park is such a temptation for me.

My mister calls this place he built Elysian Fields. Everyday hundreds of people come over here on the ferry from the city to enjoy themselves and have fun. And most of the time, that involves food. It's a chicken's paradise.

First, I always head down towards the carousel, I watch while the kids are riding around and around, and then, when it stops, I jump up and race around picking up treats as I go. You can always find kettle corn on the carousel; kids drop it as they're climbing on board a wooden horse. Sometimes I can find bits of pastry or a sausage roll. One time I was having such a good time pecking at a discarded oatmeal cookie that I got stuck on the ride and had to go around and around. I didn't like that much. When it finally stopped I was very dizzy when I hopped off and folks laughed at me as I stumbled away.

After the carousel I head over to the turtle club. Manny, the cook, always saves me some turtle feet to peck at, he even roasts them over the fire for me. Turtle feet are super tasty and since turtles have been known to attack chickens and eat them, I don't feel bad about eating their feet. Maybe if I eat a turtle's feet he won't be able to run fast enough to catch a chicken the next time he's hungry for one.

Then I head down to the path that goes through the woods. There are lots of benches and grassy areas for people to picnic and I always find the best treats there. Sometimes when families are having lunch and they see me scratching around and the children throw me pieces of their bread and cheese. Those city kids have probably never seen a chicken before and I know it's special for them to see a real live chicken in the wild, especially one as nice looking as me.

Lastly, I always head down to the cricket field. I go there because every day I'm hopeful it will live up to its name and there will be a field of actual crickets just waiting to be my lunch, so far, it's been disappointing. Maybe the crickets don't know they're supposed to gather on that field, crickets aren't the smartest bugs you will ever eat. But I go just to check it out, I would hate it if the one day I didn't go, the crickets actually showed up. But usually, it's just a group of misters hitting a ball around with a stick. How boring.

On this particular day, after I saw that there were no crickets, I decided to hang around a bit because I saw a couple of the misters eating buttered corn on the cob and I was hoping I might be able to peck at the ears when they were done. I knew those misters must have gotten that corn from Jonas the corn cob vendor. He pushed his cart around the park every day, but he always shooed me away and wouldn't share any with the chickens. He's very rude and should get some lessons from Manny the turtle soup cook about how to share with others.

As I was scratching around, I saw that the misters were even more boring today than usual. Instead of hitting the ball and running away from it as fast as they could like they usually do, they were all gathered together arguing and writing things down in a little notebook. Since I didn't want to get too far away from those corn cobs, I inched closer and listened in on their argument. It seems they were trying to come up with the rules for a new game they wanted to play called baseball. It sounded dumb. While they were discussing this one of the misters jogged out onto the field a little way and started playing catch with another mister. I guess he was tired of listening to all the talk about rules and actually wanted to start playing, I couldn't blame him.

Since it was getting late in the afternoon, I thought most folks would be done with their picnics. That's the perfect time to start scavenging around and looking for whatever food got left behind before the squirrels got to it. I don't like squirrels. But for some reason, I just couldn't give up on those corn cobs, surely those misters would be done soon. I mean, how long does it take to eat a cob of corn? I can peck every last kernel off a corn cob in no time. As I was thinking this, I was rewarded by seeing one of the men start waving his corn cob around in the face of another man as they argued about a rule for their baseball game. Suddenly, he stretched back his arm and threw that corn cob over their heads and out towards the field. I was ready. I ran between the two misters who were playing catch, straight in the direction of where it fell. I was so focused on my goal that I never even saw the ground ball that came flying at me. It bounced and hit me square in the side, the force of it made me lose my balance and tumble head over heels. I stood up, stunned, a bit shaky for a moment. Then, out of the corner of my eye, I saw a squirrel scamper down from a nearby tree and make a beeline for that corn cob! I shook the dust off my back and sprinted towards the corn, beating that squirrel to the goal by just a second or two.

Though my side was a bit sore, that corn was every bit worth the effort. I guess that mister had been so into his argument he didn't notice that he left quite a bit still on the cob. While I was enjoying my corn, I noticed that the misters had all run over and gathered around me, they were talking about me and checking to see that I was alright. I thought that was nice of them. I expected an apology from the one who beaned me with the ball, but he was too busy scribbling in his notebook to apologize.

While I was happily pecking away, I heard them saying that because of what happened to me they were going to make a new rule for their baseball game. They decided that it wouldn't be acceptable to throw the ball at another player and hit him to get him out. Out of where? I don't know. And why on earth would you *want* to purposely hit another player with a ball? I don't know that either. I just know that seeing me take that tumble and keep going inspired them to make that rule. I was proud of that, I sure didn't want anyone else to get hit by a ball, and certainly not on purpose. I guess sometimes a bad thing that happens to you can save someone else from getting hurt.

Those misters started coming regularly to our park to play their baseball game. They called themselves The Knickerbockers, which wasn't a very good name if you ask me. Soon, crowds of people started showing up to watch them play, and you know what crowds mean-snacks. Like I said, Elysian Fields is a chicken's paradise.

Robert E. Lee's Pet Chicken, Virginia, 1862

General Robert E. Lee ate my best friend. I'm so mad I haven't laid an egg in almost three days! How could a thing like this happen? Of course I know there are barbarians walking about who actually eat chickens, but I figured that only a Yankee, or a scalawag, or a republican would do a thing like that, not a Southern gentleman like Robert E. Lee! It doesn't even make sense! People are always talking about General Lee and saying how smart he is, how wise he is, how he has a great horse- well, how could someone so smart and wise and horse-loving do such an ignorant thing? I mean, doesn't he know that chickens are here on the planet to provide eggs? How can he have scrambled eggs for breakfast now that he's eaten his hen? It just isn't logical, if chickens were meant to be eaten, then why do they lay eggs? I know chickens aren't known for their critical thinking skills, but if I know that it's impossible to have eggs for breakfast without a chicken, then certainly Robert E. Lee should be able to figure that out too.

Here's how it all happened. I live on a farm with about a million other chickens. One day, my mister decided to round up a bunch of us to take over to the army camp so General Lee and the soldiers could have plenty of eggs for breakfast. Everyone knows you can't fight the Yankees unless you have a good breakfast. Well, I had a best friend named Nellie. She wasn't named Nellie when I knew her, General Lee gave her that name. See! Who eats someone who has a name? SO WRONG! Anyways, we were hatched together and grew up in the flock together. We were inseparable. We hunted pincher bugs together, scratched in the dirt together, and slept next to each other on the roost at night. The only thing we didn't do together is get captured and boxed up to go to the army. When the yard boy was grabbing chickens to shove in the boxes, I went one way and Nellie went the other. He ended up grabbing her instead of me. I was sad when I saw the wagon roll away stuffed with crates of my colleagues, I could still see Nellie's bright intelligent eyes peering at me through the slats on the crate as she rode away. At least I think it was Nellie, we all look pretty much the same, so I don't rightly know whose eyes they were.

Eventually life got back to normal on the farm, but I still thought of Nellie often. I feared that something bad had happened to her, after all, there was a war on and I knew she might have to take up arms and fight for the cause like so many others were doing.

One day I was scratching near the barn when I saw our gardener talking to a boy who comes to work on our farm from time to time when we need extra helpers. The boy was telling the most incredible story! He said that his brother was off fighting with an outfit called John Bell Hood's Texas Brigade- don't get me started about Texans, talk about barbarians... Well, his brother swore that General Lee had a pet chicken named Nellie that would sleep in his tent at night, and the boy was pretty sure it was one of the chickens that had come from our farm! He told the story like this- after our chickens arrived in camp those awful Texans pounced on them and were going to do who knows what with them when a little black hen escaped. She flew up into a tree and perched on a branch right above General Lee's tent. I knew only Nellie could be smart enough to do that! Those crazy Texans weren't dumb, so they knew not to disturb General Lee's tent, so Nellie stayed there until evening. When all the soldiers went to get their dinner, she snuck into the tent and laid an egg right underneath General Lee's cot. Nellie always laid the prettiest brown eggs; I remember because I would get jealous of hers because they were smooth and the loveliest pale brown color. My eggs are speckled and lopsided sometimes. It feels good to say that out loud, sometimes it's best to own our imperfections. Back to the story... when General Lee saw that egg and noticed Nellie sitting there, he was delighted since he had always been fond of having a pet. He was also very fond of breakfast, so he decided Nellie could stay. That's how she joined the rebel army as official breakfast provider for General Robert E. Lee.

The boy went on to describe how Nellie rode in a baggage wagon and how she was found perching in an ambulance wagon after the great battle of Gettysburg. That made sense to me, I bet Nellie tended the wounded and comforted those who were suffering in that ambulance, she was that type of chicken. She rode with the General and his army for two years before he repaid her loyalty and fidelity by eating her for dinner.

The boy said it wasn't the General's idea to eat her, his cook was the one who murdered her and cooked her up with some biscuits and gravy. The cook said there was nothing else around to eat and the General was having visitors, so he had to find something to serve them. I don't buy that because Nellie was a small hen and she wouldn't have made a big enough meal for so many people. It would have made more sense for the cook to serve them up Traveller, that's the General's horse, with some biscuits and gravy. Then they could have had all the meat they wanted because Traveller is quite a big horse. But no, that's not what happened, they ate poor Nellie, a war hero, instead of dumb Traveller, who never tended the wounded in an ambulance because he never could have fit his big, dumb self into an ambulance.

I suppose I should feel proud of Nellie for giving her life in service for the Confederacy. But I don't. I just wish she was still here scratching around in the yard with me. Why do we have to have wars? Robert E. Lee isn't the only General out there, you would think all these smart generals could get together and figure out some other way to work things out rather than by everyone killing each other. But like I said, critical thinking isn't my thing...

A Spy in the Confederate White House, Richmond, Virginia, 1865

Recently, I heard someone say, "There's something fishy going on around here." I haven't had many dealings with fish, probably because they like to stay in the water and I can't swim. On occasion though, I have had some tasty morsels of fish in the supper leftovers that the cook saves for us. Even though I haven't gotten to try a lot of fish in my life, I do enjoy a good frog now and then. Of course, chickens can't tackle a full grown frog, but those little ones are a meal all to themselves. They're entertaining to catch too as they don't go quietly. They put up quite a fuss and make a high-pitched holler when we catch them. I don't know why they do that. I eat grass all the time and it never hollers. Frogs should be more like grass.

I've been living here at the Confederate White House for years now. I like it because there's never a dull moment. There are always people milling about everywhere during the daytime, they all want to get in to see my mister, the president. While they're waiting, I like to strut around and give them something to look at. I'm quite a large rooster, and my mister calls me the "little rebel" because my feathers are Confederate gray.

People line up early in the morning and sometimes wait all day for a chance to go inside and visit with the president. If they're lucky they get to come in the house and head upstairs to his office. I have no idea why so many people want to talk to my mister all the time, but there's something called a war on, and everyone has ideas about what should be done. We're having a war because my mister, and a lot of other folks, have a dream to start their own country. Chickens don't have a lot of dreams, but I'm going to do what I can to help my mister with his.

I've never actually been inside the house, so I can't comment on what goes on in there, but you'd be surprised at all a rooster can hear just by scratching around under the windows and pecking at bugs by the rose bushes near the back porch. From what I've been hearing, my mister is worried that there's a spy inside the house. A spy is someone who finds out secrets, and then tells them to others.

Since everyone is trying to decide who the spy is, I've decided to help by narrowing down the suspects. I thought maybe one of the house helpers could be the spy. My missus calls the house helpers slaves. Since I don't know what a slave is, I just call them house helpers. At first, I thought William was the spy, he's a slave who works around the yard and does other chores. But then one day he ran off and no one has seen him since. Then, I thought it was James, who worked as a footman. Since James was a footman, he did a lot of running. He was always running beside my mister's carriage and would sometimes even run ahead of the carriage to make sure things were all arranged for wherever my mister was going that day. Well, one day, James went running and never came back. After that, I was sure it was our butler Mister Mosely. But then we had a fire in the basement and in all the commotion, Mr. Moseley went missing. I thought he might have gotten burnt up in the fire, but I think he just ran away too. I'm not sure why everyone is always running away from our house, maybe my mister should investigate that and figure out what to do about it.

So, I keep my eyes and ears open for anything that might show me who the spy is. I'm not sure how I will tell my mister once I figure it out, chickens can't talk. But I'll have to find a way. My plan is to focus only on the misters who work here. There are several missuses who work here too, but they aren't very interesting and probably aren't smart enough to be spies. I'll give you an example. One day I happened to be up on the porch railing preening my long tail feathers and making sure I was looking my best since there would be a lot of folks coming by later in the afternoon for a big reception. While I was out there a neighborhood missus knocked on the door with a basket of eggs. Since my mister and missus are very popular, people are always bringing them presents. Well, since the cook was busy, one of the maids, a missus named Missus Mary Bowser, took that basket and headed back towards the kitchen with it, only, she didn't take it to the kitchen. I saw her take it into the parlor and when she got there, she did the most curious thing. She picked up each egg and shook it hard until she found one she liked. Then she cracked that egg open right there in the parlor! I was nervous about that because my mister was in the habit of leaving his important papers all over the house and I didn't want Missus Mary to get egg all over something my mister really needed. But to my surprise, when she cracked that egg open it must have been rotten because all that came out of the shell was a piece of paper with scribbles on it! I've never seen that happen before. I don't know what kind of hens lay eggs like that. Missus Mary didn't seem upset at that rotten egg, she tucked the paper into her apron pocket, picked up the basket and brought the rest of those eggs to the kitchen like it was a perfectly normal basket of eggs. See what I mean about not being smart enough to be a spy?

There was another time that gave me even more proof that Missus Mary was definitely not the spy. Sometimes my missus's dresses needed to go to the sewing shop to be mended. One time, I was out scratching around in the backyard behind the kitchen, and I saw her sitting under a shade tree sewing a piece of paper with scribbles on it into the hem of my missus's dress! No wonder her dress needed mending, if Missus Mary was always sewing papers into the hems, my missus probably had trouble walking around with all those papers sewn all over her dress. A spy would know better than to sew papers into my missus's dresses.

After I concluded that Missus Mary was not the spy, my theory was proved by the fact that Missus Mary disappeared a few days later. I didn't think much of it though because there was a lot of commotion around town due to the fact that the war was coming to an end. Missus Mary wasn't the only one who left, my Missus and all the children left one night, the wagon packed up with their trunks and clothes. Then, my mister, President Jefferson Davis of the Confederate States of America left too. He took his papers and the Confederate gold and boarded a train out of Richmond. It's a good thing he left because that night the city caught on fire and soldiers wearing blue, not gray poured into the city.

Since I was the only one left, I knew it was my job to protect the Confederate White House. I jumped up into a tree so I could keep watch over everything. After spending the night in that tree, I decided to stay up there the next day since I was nervous about being the only Confederate chicken left in the city. That afternoon I saw soldiers accompanying a tall man with his child coming down the street. As they got closer, I recognized the tall man, I had seen his picture plenty of times on old newspapers left lying out on the porch. He was President Lincoln, and he was bringing his son to mock our empty house and laugh at our defeat. I saw them enter our house and from my vantage point in the gumtree I could see straight into the window of my mister's office. President Lincoln actually sat down at my mister's desk! I burned with anger. I determined that as soon as he came back out of the house I would jump down and spur him as hard as I could, but as I watched him closely through the window, the look on his face stopped me. He didn't look triumphant, he looked thoughtful and a little sad. That's when I realized that President Lincoln had a dream too, his dream came true, but he paid a high price for it.

That evening, I left the Confederate White House for good and headed down to a neighbor's house about half a block away. I could hear chickens clucking so I knew I would be welcome. Over the weeks to come I thought a lot about dreams and concluded that it's good to follow your dreams, but it's also OK to let go of a dream if it turns out not to be the right one. A dream that's not the right fit is a lot like that frog hollering and fussing so you can hardly enjoy eating it.

65

From that time forward I wanted my dreams to be like grass, quietly waving in the wind, just waiting for me to take a bite.

The First Egg Laid in the Klondike, Skagway, Alaska 1898

M y mister made his fortune in the Klondike Gold Rush, but he didn't make it from finding gold. He made it because of me.

I first met my mister right after I was hatched in Seattle. My mister worked for the railroad, and I guess he got a hankering for fresh eggs because he adopted me and three other young pullets. I thought I would spend my whole life in Seattle, I never knew I would end up a world traveler. But once gold was discovered in the Klondike that's where we headed.

My mister became someone they called a stampeder. That means he stampeded to the Klondike. I'm not sure what it means to stampede, all I know is we headed north in a hurry. We didn't go alone, Bessie, Jack, and Jed Tubbs went with us. Bessie and Jack are mules, Jed Tubbs is another mister. I don't like him much on account of the many times he wanted to eat me. I mean, I can forgive someone for getting hungry and maybe mentioning how tasty a chicken dinner would be, but Jed Tubbs mentioned it all the time, every day, and sometimes even more than once a day. It's a wonder I made it to the Klondike with both my drumsticks.

The first time I realized how much Jed Tubbs wanted to make a meal out of me was on the steamboat from Seattle to Skagway. As it turned out, he thought my mister was foolish for hauling chickens all the way to the Klondike. He said they had enough to carry, they didn't need to be packing chickens up over the pass. But I don't think that's the real reason he wanted to pluck me and grill me up on deck. I heard him complain that the prices in the ship's restaurant were too high. Jed Tubbs was cheap. When he noticed that my mister wasn't budging, he headed below deck to the restaurant. It didn't look to me like he missed too many meals, but I did start sleeping with one eye open from then on.

It took three days to make it to Skagway. At first, I thought we were already in the Klondike and it wasn't that bad of a trip after all. But I was wrong, the hard part was still to come. My mister loaded up all his supplies onto Jack and Bessie. He even strapped us in our crate on the top of the load on Jack's back. I appreciated getting to ride up there, we had a great view. Then we headed off on our journey over the White Pass Trail. That trail had such a pretty name that I thought it would be a pleasant journey. It wasn't. It was steep and rocky. Jack had a hard time getting over the boulders and staying on the trail. We saw a lot of horses and mules and oxen who didn't make it. It was a hard thing to see. I try not to think about it and when the memory comes to me I really quick start remembering the fat, green tomato caterpillars we had in our yard in Seattle. Sometimes it's best to think about happy things.

After we made it over the pass, I thought we were there and my mister could start stampeding. But no, we still had to float down the Yukon River. I'll tell you, if I had known there was floating involved I never would have come. Chickens can't swim and we don't like water. I especially didn't want to try and get down that river on the contraption my mister and Jed Tubbs built for us. I expected a nice ship like the one that brought us to Skagway from Seattle, but this thing they built was nothing more than a floating floor with no walls and no roof! They called it a raft and it didn't look safe at all. When my mister dragged our crate on board, we put up a fuss. That's when Jed Tubbs got a sparkle in his eye and suggested we lighten the load and celebrate making it this far with a nice roast chicken. That made me stop my fussing. I decided there were worse things than floating down the river.

When we first started out it was very pleasant and peaceful. I enjoyed listening to the water lap against the raft. I got in the habit of taking a lot of naps since there wasn't anything else to do. In fact, I was napping when we hit the rapids. You would think someone would have mentioned there were rapids! Well, our raft was tossed around on top of that water by the waves and every couple of seconds we would slam into a rock! After hitting a rather large boulder our crate came loose and we went sliding across the deck, heading straight for a watery grave. Just when we were mere inches from skidding overboard, Jack stepped on the rope that was dragging behind our crate. I would like to say that Jack did it on purpose because he wanted to save our lives, but really, I think Bessie was just crowding him a bit and he wanted to get out of her way. Then, as we were teetering on the edge with only Jack's hindleg saving us, suddenly, I saw Jed Tubbs lose his footing, fall flat on his back, and come sliding feet first down the deck towards the water! He was screeching and hollering and clawing at the air. Then, at the last second before he slid completely off and into the water, Jed Tubbs reached out and grabbed on to our crate! I guess since he couldn't have us for dinner he was bound and determined to pull us overboard with him. Now Jack's hindleg was responsible for keeping us AND Jed Tubbs, whose bottom half was dragging in the water and slamming into boulders, afloat. I guess Jed Tubbs wasn't thinking of crispy fried chicken now.

Luckily, Jack decided to keep his foot down and we made it through the rapids. My mister hauled us and Jed Tubbs back onto the raft. I kind of wished Jed Tubbs had let go and had to swim to the Klondike, but I didn't have anything to worry about. His rear end was so sore from getting smacked by boulders that he wasn't very hungry.

When we finally arrived in Dawson City my mister was a bit disappointed because by the time we got there, the gold was all gone. It seems that so many stampeders had gotten there ahead of us that they scooped up all the gold and didn't leave anything for latecomers. Kind of selfish if you ask me.

My mister was down in the dumps for a day or two, partly because there was no gold and partly because Jed Tubbs ran off with his nest egg. I was surprised when I heard that since I didn't know my mister had a nest or an egg of his own to put in it. But my mister didn't stay upset for too long before he came up with a plan. He found a large board and some paint and made a sign that said, "Com see the furst egg layd in the Klondik!" My mister wasn't great at spelling, but then, neither am I. Then he took me out of the crate and put me in a box with some old rags. We headed down to the general store and he put my box on a bench outside with that sign right next to it. Well, before you could say scrambled eggs and bacon there was a huge crowd gathered around. Folks were bored now that there wasn't any more gold to hunt for. Plus, I got the feeling that chickens were rare in the Klondike and that's why folks seemed excited to see me. They sure were patient because I can't lay an egg on demand, an egg comes out whenever it wants to come out. But sure enough, I laid an egg that afternoon in that box and the whole crowd cheered! Then my smart mister picked up that egg and sold the first egg laid in the Klondike to a well-dressed mister for five whole dollars!

After that, I laid the first egg in the Klondike about fifty times over the next few months. My mister would take me and the sign down to the wharf to meet the steamers coming in and get his five dollars from someone in the crowd as soon as I accomplished the task. I didn't mind being a working chicken, I figured I owed it to my mister for protecting me from Jed Tubbs and his appetite.

Eventually, we left the Klondike and took the steamer back to Skagway, no more floating down the river and packing over the pass for us. My mister took his new nest egg and bought a cigar store where he sells cigars, maple candy, and yes, fresh eggs. I don't lay as many eggs now as I did before since I'm getting up there in years, but I'm pretty sure my mister will keep me around since I'm the reason he's one of the wealthiest men in Alaska now. Sometimes I chuckle when I think that my mister traveled all the way to the Yukon to find his fortune in gold and ended up finding a fortune in eggs instead. I guess sometimes the most valuable things aren't things you have to go hunting for, they're the things right under your nose. Or in my case, under your bottom feathers.

Susan B. Anthony Takes a Stand, Rochester, New York, 1872

I 'm a jailbird, but that's not the worst of it. I'm also in solitary confinement. For a chicken, being in solitary confinement is more terrible than a day without grasshoppers. Chickens are very social creatures; we don't like to be alone. Since I'm the rooster of my flock I'm sure my hens are lost without me. I spend my time pacing around behind these cruel prison walls, wondering about all the things I'm missing- sunshine, sweet smelling grass, beetles... Freedom is becoming nothing more than a memory for me. I know I've only been locked up in our coop since this morning, but it seems like forever. The thing that concerns me the most is that young rooster who just hatched six months ago. I know he thinks this is his chance to take over my flock! Every time I crow to remind my hens that I'm still here, he hears me and crows right back! He mocks me with his freedom. He flaunts his good fortune with every juvenile crow that comes warbling out of his youthful beak.

All this trouble began yesterday afternoon when some men came to arrest my missus. My missus's name is Susan B. Anthony and she got in trouble because she tried to vote. Voting is when people get together and everyone says what they want. The group that has the most people who want the same thing wins, and they get to have what they want. Voting sounds like a good idea to me, in fact, if I ever breathe the sweet air of freedom again, I'm going to organize the flock so we can vote. I think we should vote for having grasshoppers for breakfast every day instead of cracked corn. That shouldn't be a problem, I've seen the man who brings the sacks of cracked corn to our barn every month, he can just as easily bring a sack of fresh grasshoppers instead of the corn, or maybe even in addition to the corn. But not brown grasshoppers, the green ones are juicer so we will definitely need to vote for green grasshoppers. I'll get right on it as soon as I get out of here.

Back to my story. My missus and some friends of hers went down to vote and they were told they couldn't vote because only misters can vote. Now why would that be? For chickens, the only difference between hens and roosters is that hens lay eggs and roosters do the crowing. Both are important jobs. In the world of misters and missuses, I'm not sure what the difference is. I don't think missuses lay eggs and I've never heard a mister crow. If anything, the missuses are definitely harder workers than the misters. The misters leave in the morning and who knows what they do all day? The missuses are busy all day feeding the chickens and baking the bread, and then giving supper scraps to the chickens, and then sweeping the floor, and then making sure the chickens have fresh water. They work so hard! I think they deserve to vote as much as the misters. That's why when those men came to take my missus away to jail, I had to do what I could to defend her.

I saw the wagon drive up and park in front of our house. When I saw the police officers get out, I knew I had to do whatever I could to help my missus. Afterall, she's a part of my flock too. The maid let them in the house, my missus was in her parlor and when I saw through the window that they intended to take her away, I knew what I had to do. I sneaked around the side of the house to the front door and hid in the azaleas by the porch. My plan was to wait for those men to come down the porch steps and then spur them as hard as I could so my missus could run away fast and hide. I crouched there as quietly as I could, I could hear my missus talking to those men in the house. My missus is a great talker, she's very smart and can talk her way into and out of things all the time. As I was listening, a honeybee started buzzing around one of the flowers and I decided a snack would help me keep my energy up while I was waiting. That bee was fast, and it took all my concentration to try and snap him up, that's why I almost missed my chance to fight for my missus. While I was busy concentrating on that bee, those men brought my missus down the steps and were taking her out to their wagon. Luckily, I'm a fast runner and I was able to burst out of the azaleas and catch up to them. Using my powerful legs, I leaped up and spurred one of them right on his rear. He let out a high-pitched yelp, turned, and when he saw me ruffling my feathers ready to have another go at him, he ran away to the safety of his wagon. I crowed in triumph, expecting my missus to praise me and dash into the house for a leftover biscuit for me as a token of her gratitude. Instead, she scolded me and told me that violence was never the answer. Then she calmly climbed up into that police wagon.

I spent the rest of the afternoon sulking by the woodpile since it was known to be the home of quite a few tasty spiders and caterpillars. I know I shouldn't use food to make myself feel better, but I couldn't help it. When I saw a carriage stop in front of our house, and my missus and her sister get out and go in, I was glad that she was OK, but my feelings were still a little hurt due to the scolding I'd received. I just didn't understand what I did wrong!

That night when my missus came down to count us and make sure we were safe for the night she looked at me and started talking. Remember what I said about my missus being a good talker? Well, she talked to me for such a long time I confess, I didn't understand a lot of what she said. This was partly because she used a lot of big words, and partly due to my being so sleepy. I think she appreciated that I wanted to help her, but she wanted me to know that missuses are strong and can take care of themselves. Then she talked a lot about the importance of women getting to vote. I got the feeling that the reason that misters don't let the women vote is because they think that women can't care for themselves and need men to take care of them. I understood that part a little, I try to look out for my hens but plenty of flocks do just fine without a rooster at all. Most of the hens I've known in my life are strong and brave and will fight to the death to protect their chicks or their home. So, I understood that this battle my missus was fighting was one I couldn't help her with, no matter how much I wanted to.

For my consequences I have been in solitary confinement in the coop all day. She doesn't seem mad at me anymore, maybe in the morning she will let me go out and be a part of the world again. I think I've learned what she wanted me to learn.

Tomorrow is a new day and I have decided to think about the hens differently, I hope I will appreciate them as equals. I hope tomorrow is a good day for my missus too. Maybe it will be the day when all the misters of the world realize that not only are women equal to them, but some women, like my missus, might even be a little bit better.

A Stop on the
Underground Railroad,
Reading, Pennsylvania, 1857

I live on the railroad. A railroad is a place where there are special houses that folks can go to in the night if someone is chasing them and they need a place to stay. I hope no one ever chases me at night. One time I was sleeping up on the roost and I felt a swoosh go right underneath me, rubbing up against my legs. When I opened my eyes, I saw it was a snake! Ever since then I've been scared of the dark.

I'm happy to live on the railroad because we're helping people. Apparently, there are a lot of people who are being treated badly. They're called slaves. Being a slave means you have to do what someone else tells you to do all day long, and sometimes they take your family away from you. I don't blame slaves for wanting to escape. I would hate it if I wasn't free, and it would be awful if someone took my chicken family away from me.

When the visitors come to our house, they're tired, scared, and hungry. My mister and missus always give them some food and clean clothes and whatever else they need. They spend a day or two with us and then head out in the night to the next railroad station. They're trying to get to a magical place called Canada where no one will chase them, and no one will make them be slaves. I wonder why Canada knows slavery is wrong, but we don't know that here in the United States?

We have visitors right now who have been here for a couple of days, a little missus and her mama. The mama is very sick, at least that's what I heard when I was scratching under the kitchen window and heard my mister talking to the doctor. The doctor always comes to help our visitors, but not everyone in town is as kind. We have to keep our visitors a secret since some people would tell the hunters about us and they would come to our house and take the visitors back to their hard lives. It could also happen that bad people would take my mister and missus away too. I heard them talking about a law that we have called The Fugitive Slave Act. It says that anyone who helps a slave can get sent away too. I don't want that to happen to my mister and missus since they are so good to us. My missus always bakes extra cornbread so there will be enough for us too because she knows that's our favorite. Cornbread is the best thing in the world. I bet the streets in Canada are paved in cornbread.

This morning, when I looked up to the top floor of the house, I saw the curtains move. I think the little missus is up there watching me. She must be bored since her mama is sick. It's possible she's watching me for another reason, lots of folks like to watch me these days because I have eight pretty chicks scratching around with me.

I enjoy being a mother, I cluck to my chicks, and I do my best to keep track of all of them while we're scratching around the yard. Sometimes it's hard to keep track of them since they do so much zooming. That's what chicks do, they zoom around. Chicks don't walk slowly, they sprint from one place to another quicker than a beetle. But they always listen to my voice and stay near me so I can take care of them. I hope seeing me with my chicks brings some happiness to the little missus, she must be awfully worried about her mama.

As the afternoon wore on and the sun got hotter, I decided to head into the barn where it was cool and maybe get a little rest. I nestled down on a big pile of hay and my chicks scooted under me. I could hear them making the happy little chirping sounds they make when they're settling down for a nap. I must have dozed off for a moment too because I was startled when I felt the hay move beside me and I opened my eyes and saw the little missus was sitting right beside me! She must have climbed out the window and down the tree next to the house just to see me. I knew it was dangerous for her to be out of the house, but I was a proud mother hen and I didn't mind showing off my babies to her. I stood up and clucked to my babies and we started scratching around right there in the hay. She smiled and clapped her hands. We were having a very nice visit until we heard an awful ruckus outside the barn. There were dogs barking and angry voices! I got scared so I squawked and herded my chicks behind a stack of hay. That little missus was scared too so she scurried back there with us, though there wasn't much room. She squeezed in behind me and I appreciated that she took such care not to step on any of my chicks. I gathered my chicks underneath me as the angry voices and barking dogs got closer.

"I don't care who you say you are, I won't allow your vicious dogs in my barn! They'll scare the milk cow so badly we won't have milk for a week!"

"I know you're hiding runaways here, and I'm not leaving until I've searched every inch of this place!" His voice was harsh and gravelly. "You think you're so clever, you think you can get away with hiding the legally owned property of others? You're breaking the law! These slaves are the lawful property of Thaddeus Brownell and I aim to bring them back to the plantation where they belong!"

"I'm aware of what the misguided laws of our country are. You can go in and have a look around if you want, but your dogs must stay out of my barn!"

I heard the man drag his dogs away. I think he must have tied them to a tree. I was glad of that, some dogs aren't used to chickens and like to chase us and I didn't want that to happen. I heard the little missus behind me sniffle, I know she was scared of those dogs too.

We sat quietly as we heard that awful man come inside the barn. I could hear his footsteps as he opened the tack room door. I heard him climb the ladder to the hay loft and poke around. I heard him jump back down, and I heard his footsteps pounding the wood floorboards as he headed in our direction... Suddenly, I felt a sharp pain on my rear end that made me screech! I jumped and twisted around. The little missus had a clump of my soft, fluffy backside feathers pinched between her thumb and finger! She yanked my feathers out!

"What was that?" the angry man growled and stomped toward the hay bales.

Suddenly, I felt another pain, even stronger than before! I squawked as loud as I could and jumped out from behind the hay.

I flapped my wings and jumped so high that I almost flew right into that ugly man's face! That little girl had done it again! I landed with a thud since chickens aren't great fliers, then went running around in circles trying to gather my chicks, who were zooming faster than I have ever seen them zoom before. Since I was fussing and squawking as loud as I could, it didn't take long before all the other hens and roosters of the farm came running to the barn, all fussing as loud as I was. Pretty soon you could hardly hear yourself think for all the racket.

"Now look at what you've done!" my mister shouted, "You've scared that poor hen half to death. Out! Get out right now before you cause any more problems!"

I think that mean mister was so startled by nearly getting smacked in the face by a chicken that he meekly turned around and followed my mister straight out of there. I was outside under the oak tree by now, catching my breath and making sure all my chicks were with me. I watched that man untie his mangy dogs and leave our property, heading down the road at quite a fast pace.

My mister watched from the yard until he was sure that man was gone, then he rushed into the barn and came back out a few minutes later with the little missus in his arms. She was crying and shaking- I knew she was as scared as I was. He took her into the house, and I hope, upstairs to her mama.

Late that afternoon, as I was resting under the holly bushes with my chicks, my mister came out and called softly for me. At first, I was a little reluctant since I was still traumatized by what had happened. Plus, my rear was sore and a bit bald from losing all those feathers. But when I saw that he had brought out a rather large piece of cornbread that he meant just for me and my chicks, I did a bit of zooming myself, because like I said, cornbread is just about the best thing ever. As I picked off small pieces for my chicks and made my clucking sound that means I have something good for them, my mister talked to me. I didn't understand all of what he said, but he seemed to be happy with me. He said I saved that little missus's life and now that her mama was somewhat better, he was going to help them move on to the next railroad station that night. He said some more things, but I was so busy eating cornbread that I didn't hear it all.

I never saw that little missus again. I hope she and her mama made it to Canada. I've forgiven her for pulling out my feathers, I know that she had to do it and even though it hurt, I'm glad I could help. When I think back to that day in the barn, I just remember how scared I was for my chicks. I would have done anything to keep them safe. But then I think of as much as I love my family, maybe there's room in my heart to love someone else too. Maybe if we're all so busy just taking care of our own, some people will get left out. What if all of us took care of our own, plus one more person, then, it seems to me, maybe everyone in the world would have someone to care for them. I think that's what the Underground Railroad is all about, making sure everyone has someone to care for them. I'm glad I got to be a part of that.

Thomas Edison Lights up a Town, Menlo Park, New Jersey, 1879

M y mister is someone people call "tenacious." I don't know what that means because chickens don't have a big vocabulary, but from what I know of him, I think tenacious means he doesn't give up. I've decided to be tenacious too.

I live on a very nice farm with a house, a barn, a chicken coop, and a large workshop for my mister and his friends to do their experiments. Right now, they're working on trying to create light. Light comes from the sun, but my mister thinks he can steal small pieces of the sun and make them go into a clear glass shaped like a pear. Then he will use long pieces of wire to give the sun a ride to the glass pears in other people's houses. At least that's my understanding of it, I'll believe it when I see it. He's been working on this for over a year now and has tried a bunch of times, some say he has tried maybe as many as a thousand times. A thousand is a big number, it's probably more than the number of eggs I lay in a week. In the summertime I sure lay a lot of eggs, not so much right now because it's cold and no one wants to lay eggs when they're cold.

So, even though my mister keeps failing in his attempts to capture the sun, he keeps trying. That's inspired me to keep working on my plan as well. You see, we have a very nice chicken coop with a large, fenced in yard to scratch around in all day. Most of the hens are perfectly happy with this arrangement, but not me. I want to explore the world outside the fence. What if there are bugs out there that I've never tasted? In the springtime I can see fields of green grass surrounding our yard. What if just beyond those fields of grass are whole fields of caterpillars? There is so much we don't know about this glorious world! I was born to be an explorer and that's what I must do.

Every day I walk the fence line testing it in places, looking for a way out. Sometimes I scratch small holes next to a high point in the fence and I can slip under and explore. Other times I flap my wings to see if I can fly up and over the fence. My missus has clipped my wings more times than I can count to try and keep me inside the yard, but the joke's on her because my feathers always grow back. My missus gets exasperated at this, she doesn't want me to be a part of the outside world, she doesn't know that I don't have a choice, I must be free! So, like my mister, I'll keep trying, no matter what. One day I'll discover a way to get out and no one will be able to stop me. I'll become famous to chickens everywhere as the hen who flew the coop and lived in the outside world! Fame drives me- fame and caterpillars.

While I work on my explorations daily, my mister continues his experiments. I know he's getting close because at night, when we're falling asleep on our roost inside the coop, I can see through the cracks in the logs that the sun is shining inside my mister's workshop even though the sky is dark outside. Sometimes people called "reporters" come to see his experiments. They want to write stories about him for the newspapers and tell the world about his experiments. But he doesn't let them stay very long. I think he doesn't want them to know that he can only capture the sun for a few minutes, the sun doesn't stay for very long in that pear shaped glass he's created. Speaking of pears, I hope the orchard has a good crop this year. Munching on pears that have fallen out of the trees is one of my favorite summertime activities.

Maybe, when I finally find a way to be free forever the reporters will come and write about me. I know the other chickens of the world will want to know how I did it, they will want to learn from me and be able to come and go as they please. Some of them will try to steal my ideas, that's why I will have to patent my discovery. I learned that word from listening to my mister talk in his workshop. Whenever I'm able to find a way out of the yard I always do my scratching under the windows of the workshop so I can hear my mister talking and learn from him. My mister says that when the light bulb (that's what he calls the sun in the glass pear) is finally done, he will need to patent his invention so others can't steal it. My mister has all the good ideas.

It's been a few weeks since I've been able to find a way out of the yard. To be honest, I haven't been trying that hard lately because it's cold and there isn't any grass anywhere and almost no bugs. But I'm still investigating weak spots in the fencing so I'm ready for spring. In the meantime, all of us are anxious to see what my mister has planned. We can see from our yard that his friends have been helping him put those glass pears up on poles all up and down our street. There's excitement in the air, I think something truly amazing is about to happen. My missus says that tonight is New Year's Eve, and my mister has a big surprise for everyone.

I tried to stay awake as long as I could, but it was hard. Chickens are good sleepers and once we fall asleep it's hard to wake us up, but I was determined. I chose a spot on the roost that was close to the small window so I could have a good view of the workshop and the street outside. I kept dozing off but was awakened from time to time by the noises of hundreds of people who had come into town on a train for the surprise. The people were dressed fancy and were in a good mood. New Year's Eve isn't a big deal for chickens, we're smart enough to know that the first day of the new year will be just like the last day of the old year, no sense in getting all worked up about it. But those people outside in the street were excited, and they sure had a reason to be.

I was dozing when suddenly all of us in the coop were awakened by the shouts from the crowd out on the street. When we opened our eyes our dumb rooster started crowing because he thought it was morning, that's how light it was outside! Every one of those glass pears on the poles were lit up! My mister's workshop was so bright it looked like the sun had left the sky and decided to live right inside those walls. It truly was remarkable, and it lasted more than a few minutes, it lasted well into the night. I don't know how long exactly because I finally fell asleep, but in the morning, we could still feel the excitement in the air even though the people were all gone.

After that folks took to calling my mister "The Wizard of Menlo Park." I don't know what a wizard is, maybe it just means a smart person because that's what my mister, Thomas Edison, is. His success has encouraged me to keep going with my plan and maybe one day people will call me "The Wizard of the Coop." All I know is that even if it does take me a thousand tries, I have to keep going. I heard my mister tell a reporter that "Genius is one percent inspiration, ninety-nine percent perspiration." I think that's a fancy way to say, never give up. And I never will.

Helen Keller Learns to Sing, Tuscumbia, Alabama, 1887

I'm egg bound, that's why I'm sitting here in a tub of warm water. Chickens aren't fond of water, that's why Noah, the yard boy, has to hold me down and keep me from jumping out. Believe me, if it weren't for Noah, I would have hightailed it out of here long ago, even though I'm feeling poorly. A while ago some of my colleagues came over to see what was happening to me. I stooped down a bit because I didn't want them to think I was trying to be a duck. No one likes ducks.

Being egg bound means there is an egg inside of me that won't come out. Laying an egg is a relatively simple thing to do, but not laying one can be deadly. I don't know why this has happened to me, it's not like I'm not trying to lay this egg, it just won't come out no matter what I do. A few months ago this happened to another hen and she died. I don't want that to happen to me, so I'm tolerating Noah holding me in this warm water, he must think it will help me, I hope it does.

Off in the distance I can see a new missus walking around with the little missus. They call the new missus "teacher." I think a teacher is someone who shows other people how to do things. We have an old hen in our flock who thinks she's a teacher. She's always butting in when I'm scratching around like she wants to teach me how to do it, please! I was born knowing how to scratch! But as I sit here neck deep in water, watching all that's going on around me, I'm glad that the teacher is here for the little missus. The little missus needs someone to help her.

I remember a time when I was still young, our missus brought the little missus down to the barn to visit the animals. She used to do that from time to time, I think she thought the little missus would enjoy petting the animals, but the little missus didn't seem to enjoy doing anything. She was always so angry. That was a terrifying day for all of us in the barn. The little missus wasn't gentle, she pulled the goat's tail so hard I heard him bellow in pain. Then, when the donkey wouldn't lower his head enough so she could pet him, she kicked him hard in the leg. When the missus took her over to the barn cat's litter, I was seriously worried for the kittens, they weren't much older than I was, and I thought the little missus might hurt them. When she picked one up, she picked it up from its tail end instead of its head end, it was almost like she didn't know which end was the best end. That's when I realized the little missus was blind.

Not being able to see must be hard. How could I catch a cricket if I couldn't see? How would I know when it was time to go into the coop at night to sleep if I couldn't see? I think it would make me scared, scared and angry.

When I saw the teacher start to walk the little missus towards us, I got a little panicky and tried to jump out of the tub, but the water had soaked my feathers and I was a lot heavier than I usually am. Plus, Noah is very strong. He spends his days in the garden, taking care of the plants is hard work. As they got closer, I let out my warning screech. Chickens do a lot of talking to each other. We have our own language with a sound for everything. When a predator approaches we have a sharp cackle we make to let everyone know that there's danger around. We have a high-pitched cluck when we're angry and a low-pitched cluck when we want to gather our chicks underneath us for the night. But my favorite sound that we make is our egg song. When we lay an egg, we start to sing about it. I'm not sure why we do it, maybe just to announce to the world the great thing we've just accomplished. As I sat there in that tub of water, I sure wished I had a reason to sing my egg song.

When they got to the tub I let out another panicked screech but the little missus didn't seem to hear me. She slammed her hand hard on my back and splashed water all over my head. She grabbed me with one hand around my neck and started to squeeze the life out of me, I couldn't even get enough breath to let out a warning cluck. Noah used his free hand to help the teacher get the little missus to let me go. She was angry when they made her let go, I don't think she wanted to hurt me, I just don't think she knew what she was doing. That's when I noticed that everything the little missus touched, the teacher would make movements into her hand. I've never seen anyone do that before, but I watched her make those movements in her hand and the movements were different when she touched the water, and different when she touched Noah. Then the teacher made the little missus touch me and made different movements in her hand for me. For a moment I wondered why she was making those movements, why didn't she just tell the little missus our names? Then it occurred to me, maybe the little missus couldn't hear, either.

I breathed a little easier when the teacher led the little missus away. It was a hot day and I watched them head towards the water pump. I watched as the teacher tiredly pumped water and made movements in her hand. Suddenly, the little missus got very still and her face changed. I've watched her all my life and trust me, she's never still. She reached out and as the water splashed over her fingers, she grabbed the teacher's hand and made her make the movements into her hand again. That's when I saw something I have never seen before, the little missus smiled. Not just a regular smile, but a smile that burst out of her like it had been pent up inside- a smile that had waited her whole life to arrive. I realized that the movements the teacher was making with her hands were a language, and that for the first time in her life, the little missus was learning to speak. And as I watched our little missus laugh and grab the teacher to hug her, I felt the egg inside me shift.

I watched as our mister and missus ran from the house to hold their little missus in their arms. As they hugged her the little missus reached out and her teacher made the special movements in her hand that meant "mother" and "father." It was like looking at a different person, so bright and shining was the look on our little missus's face when she learned that everyone she loved had a name.

Later that evening, as everyone was settling down to sleep, I sat down on a pile of hay in the corner of our barn and laid that egg. I was exhausted and weak, but so relieved that I quietly sang out my egg song. Even though everyone was trying to sleep, no one protested. I think they were happy because the song meant I would live. As I looked through the door of the coop I could see the shadows falling across the lawn. I saw Noah heading towards the barn to shut us safely in for the night. Just beyond him I could see a light on in the little missus's room. She was there with her teacher and everything she held up, from her doll to her pillow, the teacher spelled a word into her hand. She was so happy that if chickens could smile, I would have smiled for her. For her whole life the little missus had a song inside her that wouldn't come out, and now, she's finally learned to sing.

Teddy Roosevelt's White House Menagerie, Washington D.C., 1903

I live at the White House, but it isn't really any big deal, it's just a place like any other place. I'm not one to brag. Besides, I'm not the only chicken here, there's a one-legged rooster who lives here too. I don't know why, but everyone is always going on and on about him. Whenever folks come to visit, they're always pointing at him and talking about him. Honestly, having one leg isn't a big accomplishment or something, I don't know why people like him so much, I'm way more interesting.

My name is Baron Spreckle. My mister is Teddy Roosevelt, the President of the United States of America. Being president is a very important job, I know that because I'm a president too. I'm the self-appointed president of the animal population of the White House. Technically presidents should be elected to office in a democratically run election, but animals are busy creatures and since we haven't had time for voting, I just went ahead and appointed myself president. I'm not sure the other animals know that I'm their president, but they'll know soon enough. Something very important is about to happen that will make me even more famous than one-legged rooster.

Most people don't know that there are more animals here at the White House than there are people. That's because my mister has a lot of kids, and those kids have a lot of pets. I don't like all the pets, but I understand that to be their leader I have to rule them with fairness and integrity even if I don't like them. That's the president's job. I won't have any problem ruling my friends, namely the parrot, Loretta, and Eli Yale, a fancy bird called a macaw. I think the fact that we all have feathers creates a special bond between us. Plus, since Eli Yale and Loretta can talk, they're going to teach me to talk too. Once I'm a talking chicken I may even be more popular than the president himself!

The other pets aren't aware yet that I'm in charge, but I think the best way to show them will be to get a stick. My mister always says, "speak softly and carry a big stick." That's what I plan to do. Carrying a stick may be difficult because I don't have hands, I will have to carry it in my beak. That's OK because the "speaking softly" part is kind of hard too since I don't really know how to talk yet. Maybe if I have that big stick in my beak no one will notice that I can't talk. Besides, a good leader doesn't have to talk all that much, just set a good example and that's what I aim to do.

Other than the parrots, Eli Yale, and the one-legged rooster, the rest of my constituents all have fur, not feathers. I try not to think less of them for that. There's a bunch of guinea pigs, but they aren't very intelligent and don't do much but sit around and wiggle their noses all day. There are several snakes that I'm not too fond of since snakes like to eat eggs and that's just rude. There's a badger that I keep clear of since he's mean and looks at me like I'm a potential meal. Of course, there's a bunch of dogs and cats, and a couple of rabbits. There's also a lizard that looks tasty, but I think my presidency might be frowned on if I eat one of the folks I'm pledging to protect. All in all, there's quite a few animal Americans that will be looking to me for leadership, once they know I'm their leader.

So, how will they know that I'm their leader? Well, a very big thing is about to happen, I heard a couple of the kids talking about it. Apparently, the public is fascinated with my mister's love of animals and a toymaker is busy making a surprise for my mister and the public. All we know is that it will be a stuffed version of one of my mister's favorite animals. Well, it simply has to be me! Why else would my mister give me an important name like Baron Spreckle? That one-legged rooster doesn't have a name! The rumor is that the toy maker is going to name the stuffed animal after my mister, that means it will be called a Teddy Chicken! Can you imagine? Every child in America will go to bed at night with a stuffed toy version of me in their arms! Soon the whole world will want one! The Teddy Chicken will be the most popular toy ever created. When that happens, even that mean badger will have no choice but to validate my presidency.

While I'm waiting for this big thing to happen, I'm busy learning all about government by listening to my mister when he talks to his important friends out on the White House porch. They like to drink coffee and talk about the things they want to see happen in America. My mister is very smart and his idea is to create something called a "Square Deal." This Square Deal is a plan to make sure everyone is treated fairly no matter how rich or poor they might be. It means everyone should have equal chances in life. I think that's a good policy for me to adopt as well. Even though the Guinea pigs aren't super bright, they should still be given the chance to do whatever it is that Guinea pigs want to do, in a fair and equal manner. My mister also says that the Square Deal will make sure that people are paid equally and that they are treated right in their jobs. That means I'll get a bit of extra recognition because I produce eggs for the family. None of the other animals around here do anything productive. Finally, the Square Deal ensures that the outdoor spaces will be preserved so everyone can enjoy them for generations to come. I like that because we have quite a nice lawn here at the White House and I have eaten my share of fat worms from that lawn. It's nice to know that the lawn will be protected, and the worms will not run out.

While I was thinking about all this my mister's noisy kids came running out onto the porch with a box a messenger must have sent over. Since they were excited about whatever was in that box, I decided to jump up on the porch and have a look. I heard the kids chattering about the toymaker finishing that special stuffed animal and I perked right up. It was finally time to see myself as the Teddy Chicken! I was so excited I relieved myself right there on the porch, but no one noticed because they were hauling those stuffed animal toys out of the box and passing them around. Everyone was laughing and talking excitedly. I finally got close enough to see the Teddy Chicken, and to my dismay, it wasn't a chicken at all! It was a stupid brown bear! A Teddy Bear? Whoever heard of something so dumb! What child could possibly ever want one of those? As I listened to the excited chatter, I heard the story of why the bear was chosen. Apparently, on my mister's last hunting trip someone wanted him to shoot a bear and he refused, so now everyone thinks bears are his favorite! That's so not fair! I'm the one who has a giant egg pass out of my body every other day just so the president can have an omelet for breakfast twice a week! I'm the one who keeps the lawn free of grasshoppers so they don't jump up and get tangled in the children's hair!

I was so disgusted with it all that I hopped off the porch and walked around to the lawn to see if a snack would make me feel better. Why couldn't everyone just see things my way? It occurred to me that maybe I wasn't cut out to be president. A true president wouldn't get offended just because they didn't get a toy created for them. I should be happy for the bear, not jealous. It made me think of something I once heard my mister say, "Do what you can, with what you have, where you are." When I first heard that I didn't understand what he meant. Now I think he meant that you don't need titles, you don't need everyone to follow you and pay attention to you. Anyone can make a difference. Maybe I was looking at things all wrong. I was so concerned with being in charge I wasn't thinking of others. We can all make a difference; we don't need to be a president in order to do something that matters. That one-legged rooster was making folks happy just by hopping around! He was doing what he could, with what he had, where he was. So maybe I ought to be a little more like that rooster, at least, I think that's what my mister would say.

The Ringling Brothers Start a Circus, Baraboo, Wisconsin, 1889

I 'm seriously considering running away from home to join the circus. I know that sounds drastic, but I was born for greatness, and I'll never find it scratching around here in the backyard. Yesterday a wagon stopped in front of our house and plastered on the side of it was a huge banner advertising "Mabel, the Hoop Jumping Leghorn." Mabel used to live here with us before she joined the circus and got her face on a banner. That should be me on that banner, not Mabel! I know I had my chance, but doesn't everyone deserve a second chance? Running away is my only option.

If I run away to the circus, I think I can make it. It will be a long and difficult journey. I won't have time to rest, and I won't be able to carry food and water with me. I'll be at the mercy of the weather and who knows what kind of predators will come after me, but it's simply a risk I must take. I've never walked three blocks before, but with a good breakfast, perhaps I'll survive. If I start to faint, maybe I can catch a grasshopper on the way for a snack to give me the energy to keep going. I must make up my mind soon if I'm really going to try. The circus will only be here in town for the winter, in the spring they'll pack up and head out to tour the world and I'll be left behind, again.

You may wonder how I have so much information on the comings and goings of the circus. Well, that's because my mister is one of the owners of the circus. His name is Al Ringling and he and his brothers started the circus a long time ago, before I was hatched. My mister is very smart and can do incredible things. Not only does he keep the circus organized, but he performs in it too. He can do lots of tricks like balancing on wires and boards. He can also juggle all sorts of things. One time he came out to our nesting boxes, gathered up a bunch of eggs, and then started throwing them around in the air and catching them! It made me nervous to see my eggs go flying around like that. It takes work to lay an egg and I don't think they should be tossed around. People should sit down at a beautiful table with a white tablecloth with candles and flowers in the center of the table as they slowly eat one of my delicious eggs. At least that's what I think.

That's how I know about the circus. How I know about Mabel is because I actually know Mabel. She lives here in the wintertime when the circus isn't traveling. In fact, Mabel and I were hatched together so I've known her my whole life. I wish I could say she was mean and selfish, but she isn't. Fame hasn't gone to her head- yet.

Mabel got her start with the circus about a year ago. We were still pullets then. My missus came out to the yard with a couple of big wooden hoops and a pocket full of treats. Chickens will eat just about anything when it comes to treats. If I remember correctly, on that day she had some pancakes that were left over from breakfast in her pocket. Everyone enjoys a good pancake. She pulled over an old bench and nailed a wooden hoop to the center of the bench, so it was standing up straight. Then, she picked us up one at a time and set us down at one end of the bench. She dropped a piece of pancake on the bench just past the hoop so you would have to go through the hoop to get it. That was no problem, anyone can do that, especially when pancakes are involved. It was the next part that was tricky. Once you got to the end of the bench, she held out the second hoop, even with the bench. It was far enough away from the edge of the bench that you would have to jump off the bench, flap your wings and fly through the hoop, and land on the ground to get your next piece of pancake. Now I ask you, why would anyone do that when they could simply jump off the bench and run around the hoop to get the pancake? It's quicker and a more efficient use of energy. And that's just what I did. I saw my missus shake her head slightly and make a clicking sound with her tongue, and just like that, my future in the circus was over.

The only one of us who jumped through the hoop was Mabel. Of course, her name wasn't Mabel then, none of us had names. I'm not sure if Mabel was just smarter than us and she knew that jumping through that hoop would make her famous, or if she was dumber than us and really saw no other way to get a piece of pancake. But either way I guess it doesn't matter, because now Mabel's a star and I'm not.

Back to my plan, I know that once I've walked the three blocks and arrived at the lot and barns where all the circus animals and folks are resting for the winter, I will have to have something to offer if I want my chance to be a star. I'm not much to look at, I'm an ordinary brown hen, not a fluffy white hen like Mabel. So, my looks won't get me far. I will have to rely on my talent. The problem is I don't have any. I've watched my mister as he practices his tricks, I can't do the egg juggling thing because I don't have hands. My only hope is to learn to balance. Specifically, I will have to learn to walk on the tightrope.

The tightrope is just that. A rope tied between two trees very tightly so you can walk across it and jump up and down on it and do whatever other crazy things you want to do. My mister has a tightrope here in the backyard where he practices from time to time. It's about five feet off the ground, so with a mighty jump and a lot of flapping I can make it up there, but once I get there, I have a hard time staying there. I've tried it a million times, I can clutch the rope easily, it's just a lot thinner than our wooden poles in the roost. It's also slippery. The first time I tried it I was determined to hang on tight and try and slide my way down to the other end. But the rope was a bit bouncy and though I had a good grip on it, I lost my balance and ended up hanging upside down. Then I didn't know what to do. I flapped my wings as hard as I could, but I couldn't get myself right side up again. I was pretty determined and hung there for quite a while, partly because I wanted to get upright, partly because I didn't want to fall off and land on my head. But eventually my strength ran out and I had to let go. I was able to tuck my head so I landed more on my back than my head. Luckily it was pretty grassy, so I didn't get hurt. But it was embarrassing because everyone was staring at me, even Mabel.

So, as I headed out for one more try on the tightrope, I didn't feel very hopeful. In fact, once I got close to it, I just didn't have the heart to try again. I knew nothing had changed and I would just end up hanging upside down, a laughingstock for all to see. I lowered my head and turned away. It's hard to give up on a dream. I decided to just spend some time alone, mourning the loss of my future in the circus.

I wandered over to the other side of the tree that holds one end of the tightrope. There's a swing that the children, when they were young, used to use from time to time there. Just an ordinary wooden plank held by two ropes tied high up in the branches. I jumped up on the swing and settled in. The force of my jump made the swing do what it does best- swing. It was a peaceful place to think about life and the chances that had passed me by. So peaceful in fact, that I tucked my head under my wing and dozed off.

When I woke up, I was surprised to see both my mister and missus standing a few feet away from the swing, staring at me and talking excitedly. I heard my missus say, "We can call her Henrietta, the Swinging Hen!" Then my mister said, "That's perfect! We can put her right next to the Strongman and the Bearded Lady! She'll be a hit!" Then, to my utter surprise, my missus pulled out of her pocket an entire pancake, the whole thing! She set it gently on the seat next to me and watched me as I gobbled it up while the swing kept swaying back and forth.

I guess just when things look the darkest, there's always hope that something great can happen. It may not be what you thought would happen, or even what you always dreamed would happen. But it can still be something great, just the same.

George Washington Carver and the Peanut Experiment, Tuskegee, Alabama, 1899

I go to college. I'm proud to be one of the few chickens who go to college. I like college so much that I attend classes every day. For my first class of the day, I go around to the back of the college cafeteria because the cooks sometimes throw away leftover dinner scraps and then I can help myself. Next, I go to home economics. That's where we learn to cook. I don't actually learn, I just hang out under the window and sometimes someone inside will want me to taste test their project, so they toss me a piece out the window. After home economics it's lunch time, so I go down to the college picnic areas where all of us students have lunch. I don't bring my own lunch because my classmates like to share theirs with me. They throw me a crust from their sandwiches or sometimes an apple core. I love apple cores. At times I will get more than just the core because someone will throw me a whole apple, just because it has soft spots. I don't know why some folks don't like mushy apples, I think that's the best kind of apple! For my last class of the day, I go to the agriculture department. It's an outdoor garden where we grow all sorts of things. It's my favorite class because I learn a lot about which bugs and plants taste the best. Sometimes my professor doesn't appreciate me tasting a bug or plant that he's studying, but he understands that he can't quench my thirst for knowledge. In fact, I think I will major in agriculture and dedicate my life to tasting every plant and bug in the whole world, well, at least every plant and bug in the whole of Alabama.

My agriculture professor is a good mentor for me, I'm pretty sure I'm his favorite student. His name is Professor George Washington Carver and he likes to do experiments with plants. He wants to teach people how to grow things in large quantities, and because of that, he needs an assistant who can eat large quantities of food. That's me.

Professor Carver has a dream to improve the lives of his people by teaching them the best ways to grow things. Apparently, there's more to it than just digging a hole and tossing a seed in the ground. I think the best thing to grow is tomatoes, but unfortunately, my professor is focused on peanuts and sweet potatoes. There's nothing wrong with peanuts and sweet potatoes, it's just hard for me to help myself to them because they grow under the ground. I'm a good scratcher and I like to dig holes for dust baths, but digging for peanuts and sweet potatoes is a lot of work and therefore, not the best use of my time. I think this is probably true for most folks, I wish I could get the professor to see that so he would stop wasting time and start concentrating on easier crops like grapes, lettuce, and tomatoes - especially tomatoes. Sometimes giant, green caterpillars like to live on tomatoes so you can get two food groups at once. I think that's a valuable discovery of mine, if I knew how to write, I would write a paper about it.

Another important mister around here is the head of my university. His name is Professor Booker T. Washington. He comes to the agriculture department sometimes to check on what we're doing. Sometimes he shoos me away from the garden, but that's only because Professor Carver hasn't gotten around to telling him that I'm his best student. Professor Washington built this university from the ground up, and I mean that literally. I hadn't hatched yet so I didn't see it for myself, but apparently Professor Washington and his students actually built the buildings where our classes are held. He contacted people to help with the funding for the college and recruited the teachers like Professor Carver. Maybe someday I will be recruited to be a teacher here. I would enjoy teaching a class about tomatoes.

My academic career was going very well until I started to disagree with the goals of the experiments we were conducting. I know it's common for brilliant minds to sometimes disagree, but I'm sad to say that I think Professor Carver has gone a little off the deep end. He's been doing a lot of experiments for alternative uses for peanuts. He seems to think we can do more with peanuts than just eat them. Personally, I think eating them is enough, I mean, what's more important than food? But he's found ways to turn peanuts into all sorts of things such as shampoo and soap! Honestly, who wants to slurp down some shampoo or munch on a bar of soap? That doesn't sound tasty at all. I was willing to just chalk that up to a difference of opinion (speaking of chalk - peanut chalk!), but when he decided to make sweet potatoes into vinegar, shoe polish, and paint, that's where I had to draw the line. I'm not eating paint. I thought our goal was to help farmers improve their lives by growing successful crops. What farmer is going to feed his child shoe polish? I'm so glad he never got excited about growing tomatoes. What if he came up with the crazy idea to smash tomatoes up into a liquid and then dip fried potatoes in it or something? That would be a heartbreaking waste of a good tomato.

So, I've decided to give up my career in academics. I'm now a college dropout. I briefly thought about organizing a student demonstration to protest the misguided use of perfectly good produce. I know that as an American I have the right to peaceably assemble and make my grievances known. I learned this in my history class while I was lurking outside the window eating a half a peanut butter sandwich a classmate tossed to me. Peanut butter- oh the irony! But since I am no longer a student, I know it's time to get a job and become a productive member of society. I'm not sure what job I'm best suited for, maybe something in the tomato growing industry. Or maybe as a professional food taster. Or perhaps I should just head back to the coop and lay an egg. Maybe that's the job I was born to do. A college education is all fine and dandy, but honest work is honest work. At least that's what I think.

Belle Boyd Spies for the South, Front Royal, Virginia, 1862

I 'll never forget the day that gray, speckled hen came to live with us. Her feathers were a dark gray, almost blue and she had a lovely pattern of white streaks around her neck. My missus named her Sasha and thinks she's the prettiest hen she's ever seen. She always calls out to her and says, "How's my prettiest little girl today?" Really? How is that supposed to make the rest of us feel? I'm just a plain, old brown hen. No one has bothered to give me a name, but Sasha shows up and everyone gushes over her like she's the queen of the coop or something. I hate her.

As it turns out, hating someone takes a lot of energy and I would rather use my energy to chase fast-moving beetles. I don't like the slow, pokey beetles, they taste sour. The fast-moving ones are fun to catch and taste like my favorite supper scraps- mashed potatoes and gravy. Sometimes I wonder why my missus doesn't just forget about wasting time mashing potatoes and just serve up some fast-moving beetles for supper. But my mister is tired when he gets home from work and probably isn't in the mood to chase a beetle around the supper table. Mashed potatoes and gravy just sit there and are easier to eat.

The funny thing is, as time went on, I began to consider Sasha my friend. She was always wanting to scratch around with me and sometimes she would even let me eat first and get the best supper scraps. I appreciated that. That's why when I decided to sit on eggs, I didn't suspect anything when she started sleeping in the nesting box next to me. I thought she was just being friendly, and since it was chilly outside, my eggs and I appreciated the extra warmth she provided. I didn't know then what I know now.

On the night my eggs began to hatch I was completely happy. I could feel them moving under my feathers and every now and then I could hear a faint chirp coming from inside one of the eggs. I made soft clucking sounds to encourage them to keep pushing their way out of the shells. I stayed awake as long as I could but sleep finally overtook me and I dreamed about how wonderful it was going to be to be a mother.

The next morning when I woke up, I was very surprised to not feel anything at all underneath me. Where were all my eggs? Where were my chicks? It didn't take long to find them, they were all hatched and sitting happily under Sasha! Sasha stole my babies! She must have waited for me to fall asleep before stretching her neck underneath me and rolling my eggs out one by one. I was so infuriated I could hardly be civil! I turned my head to give her a big peck, but she had already gotten up. She took my seven lovely chicks and headed out of the barn to give them their first lesson in scratching. I was left with empty shells. I was back to hating Sasha.

Maybe it was because of what happened to me that the minute Missus Belle Boyd came to stay with us I knew right away that she was a sneak just like Sasha. She was my missus's niece, but my missus was sweet and kind, Belle was selfish and untrustworthy. I noticed it right away. Sometimes a mister would come to our house for a visit and Belle would meet him on the porch and bat her eyes at him and hang on to his sleeve. She would talk him into telling her secrets, and then, late at night, she would tiptoe into the barn and saddle a horse and ride away with those secrets, looking for someone to tell. She just pretended to like those misters so they would tell her things, just like Sasha pretended to like me so she could steal my babies. If I had a whole bucket full of fast moving beetles I wouldn't share them with either of those two sneakers!

Eventually I realized that Belle had a good reason for gathering all those secrets. Our town had become overrun by Union soldiers, and they were about as welcome in Front Royal as Sasha was welcome in the barn. Belle Boyd had decided to do her part to send those soldiers packing.

One night, some important soldiers came to our house to stay. They decided to have a meeting in one of the rooms and tell each other secrets. Since Belle loved secrets, she wanted to get those secrets from those misters. She went into a closet upstairs that happened to have a small hole in the floor. I know this because I often heard my missus complain about that hole because sometimes spiders would drop down that hole and land in her lap while she was doing her sewing in the room below. I'm not sure why this upset my missus, sewing is a lot of work, and you would think a snack that drops in your lap while you're working would be a welcome thing, but not for my missus. She was always nagging my mister to fix that hole. Well, Belle knelt on the floor of the closet and spied on those Union soldiers as they sat around telling secrets. Then she quietly came down the stairs, headed out to the barn, and saddled up old Blossom, our mule. I don't know where she went that night, but I'm pretty sure she delivered those secrets to someone who needed them because several weeks later, the war between the states came to the streets of our town!

I tried to go about my business as usual, but it was hard with soldiers running around everywhere and cannons booming in the distance. What made it even harder was when I almost got trampled by Missus Belle Boyd as she decided to run wildly out of our house and head out to the battlefield. At first, I thought she was going to church because she had on a fancy white dress, I thought church would be a good place for her since she was always tricking misters and breaking hearts. But when I saw her take off her bonnet and start waving it out where the misters were busy shooting at each other, I knew she was up to something. I found out later that she had a secret that she was just busting to tell the Confederate general and she didn't care if she got shot in the process.

Some days later I heard Missus Belle telling a group of ladies that she almost perished on the battlefield, she said that her pretty white dress was full of bullet holes that were meant to end her life. I rolled my eyes when I heard that. I like to scratch under the laundry lines because it's shady there and I saw her dress hanging out to dry, I didn't see any bullet holes. But I think telling wild stories was just part of who Missus Belle was- people seemed to like hearing her tales.

Eventually those soldiers took Missus Belle away to prison, but from what I heard, she didn't stay there long. She was back to her old tricks as soon as she was released. It was probably a disappointment to her when she heard that my mister nailed a board over that peephole in the upstairs closet so the spiders can't drop on my missus any more.

As for Sasha, I've decided to forgive her for stealing my babies. After what I've seen in this war, I know that hating someone can be an ugly thing. I think Sasha has decided to make peace with me too, but I still get up and head for another nesting box when she slides in next to me. I can forgive, but do I really have to forget?

The Statue of Liberty Comes to America, Bedloe Island, New York, 1886

I live on an island of misters, which is fine with me since I'm a mister myself. In the chicken world, misters are called roosters. Everyone knows that roosters are superior to hens, I think it's the same with folks. Misters are definitely better than missuses. I've only ever met two missuses in my whole life, and I wasn't impressed by either of them. One was the mother of one of the soldiers who live here. She came to visit her son and the whole time she was here all she did was nag him. She told him his hair was too long, he was looking too skinny, he should be married by now, and on and on and on. I could tell that poor mister was happy to see her go. The other missus was the sweetheart of one of the soldiers and all I remember about her is that she was pretty much helpless. She needed help getting off the boat, she needed help walking over the rocks, she needed her mister's coat when it started raining- she was a lot of work. So, you can see why I was disappointed when I found out that the massive statue we are building turned out to be a missus!

The statue is a gift to us from a place called France. I never want to go to France because apparently, they have gigantic missuses there. This missus we are building is so big that one of her toes is large enough to squish me flat if she were able to step on me. I bet all the chickens in France live in fear of getting stepped on all the time. Another problem with her is she has a big book in one of her hands. Everyone knows that nothing good comes from reading. In her other hand she has a torch with fake flames. Why does she need a torch in the daytime? It's suspicious. I won't be deciding to visit France anytime soon.

So, for now, I spend my days scratching around with the rest of our small flock. We like to head over to the statue at lunchtime because the workers will sometimes share parts of their lunches with us. Some of the workers sure are brave, they've had to hoist the pieces of that missus high into the air to put the statue together. They also had to find the right pieces because that gigantic missus got delivered to us from France in about a million wooden crates. The least they could have done was deliver her already assembled. So rude.

Now that the statue is done the preparations are underway for the big celebration tomorrow. Early in the day misters will start arriving on the island for the unveiling of the statue's face. I've heard that more than two thousand misters will be here, and almost no missuses. That's for the best since, as I've already pointed out, missuses would probably just ruin the day anyways.

With all the commotion at the statue we've decided to do our scratching down by the rocks on the other side of the island. Our mister, who runs the kitchen for the garrison, doesn't care where we go for the day. As long as the hens lay their eggs in the morning, we can wander anywhere we want. I like to take my flock down by the water because there are small crabs to catch and sometimes, we can even find an oyster with a crack that we can peck at enough to get the shell off. Oysters are tasty.

While we were down by the water, I found a small pool that had some minnows swimming around in it. Minnows are fun to catch, so I clucked to get some of the hens to come over and admire what I had found for them. It's because I had my back turned that I didn't see the osprey coming. An osprey is a bird that likes to fish, so usually they aren't a predator for us because we aren't fish, but on this particular day, a hen with several chicks had accompanied us down to the rocks. I guess the sight of those chicks was too much for that osprey to ignore. I heard the hen screech and turned just in time to see that the osprey, with its talons outstretched, was about to snatch one of those chicks away from its mother. I was so scared that I did what any normal chicken would do, I started to run away, but that mama hen wasn't going to go without a fight. She jumped between the osprey and her chick and took the full brunt of those talons. That osprey couldn't stop in time and hit her on the back with its razor-sharp claws. The hen turned and started fighting furiously, defending her chicks with all her might.

At this point I finally came to my senses and shook off my fear. I knew it was my job to protect my flock, so I ran back and entered the fight. Roosters have long, sharp spurs, hens don't have spurs, so that poor mama hen was at a disadvantage when it came to fighting off seabirds. I leaped in with no thought to myself and spurred that osprey as hard as I could. It didn't take long before the osprey decided that a fish dinner was less painful than a chicken dinner. It flew away dripping blood from a nasty cut I gave it on its underbelly.

As I watched that osprey fly away, I tried to crow in triumph, but I was consumed by shame. It was my job to protect the flock and at the first sign of trouble I cowered. I looked at the mama hen and saw that she was bleeding badly from the cuts on her back, but she seemed not to notice. She clucked and clucked, intent on calling every one of her chicks back to her from where they had scattered. As we all headed back to safety, I tried to stay close to that hen, I felt bad that I had run and was hoping that no one noticed. I think that's when my opinion of missuses began to change.

The next day that hen decided to rest in our coop with her babies, I thought that was a good idea, but I wasn't about to miss the show. Already there were huge crowds of misters on the island, I even got a glimpse of President Grover Cleveland as he arrived and disembarked from the ferry that brought him from the city. All around our island, in the harbor there were hundreds of boats. People were sailing around, all excited to see the celebration of the gigantic French missus.

As we scratched around from a distance, I looked and looked, and sure enough, I didn't see a single missus in the crowd. I heard afterwards that among the two thousand people who visited our island that day, they were all misters except for two missuses who were related to important misters. I don't know why that bothered me, but it did.

Soon, we could hear the president's voice booming as he gave a speech. He talked about freedom and liberty and how that gigantic French missus was a symbol of what America wanted to be. While he was speaking, I glanced out at the harbor and saw a boat filled with missuses. I knew they were upset because they hadn't been allowed to come to the celebration, but more than that, they were upset because they weren't treated as equal to the misters. Some of them had signs that protested that they didn't have the right to vote. I'm not sure what voting is but from seeing how sad those missuses on the boat were, it seems like it must be important. As I watched them on their boat, I remembered that hen who jumped in to do what should have been my job and I knew they were right. Missuses were strong and brave, they deserved to have the same rights as misters.

That day, the misters celebrated a missus as a symbol of American freedom but didn't invite the missuses of America to be a part of it. Even a rooster, with a brain smaller than an acorn, can see that those misters were wrong. It took an osprey to change my mind about missuses, I wondered what it would take for everyone else.

The Yankee's Secret Weapon, Corinth, Mississippi, 1862

E verything was fine around here until those Yankees showed up. I've tried to be open minded and accept new things, but Yankees make that hard to do. I don't even know where to start...

Ever since they started wandering around, all the chickens have had to be penned up under the porch. My missus says we have to stay hidden because if the Yankees see us, they will want to catch us and eat us. Are you kidding me? Eat us? What kind of barbarians are they! Down here in the South we certainly don't eat each other, we're civilized. In fact, now that I think about it, every now and then I notice one of the chickens from our flock is missing. Usually, it's a young rooster. I'll bet those Yankees have been lurking around our farm for years, kidnapping us and eating us!

The Yankees are here because of the war. The war seems to be all about who gets to boss who around. They're in a fight over our town because they hate trains and don't want trains to pass through

Corinth. Um, what? Why can't trains go where they want to go? The Yankees aren't the boss of them.

On the first day of the battle we watched it all unfold from our prison under the porch. Since our house is about a mile from town, we were right in the middle of it. We could see the blue coats running furiously through the fields next to our barn, and sometimes they ran through our yard so close I could have reached out and pecked them if I wanted to. We hunkered down in the darkest corner under the porch because I was sure all that running would make them hungry and I was concerned those chicken eaters would see me and decide that it was supper time. Our dog Max stood at the fence line barking his head off at all the action. I was worried about him because for all I knew, Yankees might eat dogs too. I wouldn't put it past them.

What I remember most about that day was the noise. We could hear shouting, and shots cracking through the air. We heard the booming of cannons being fired and the rumble of horse's feet as they pounded through the yard and leaped over the fence next to our coop. War sure is a noisy business. For a while, things seemed to quiet down a bit, but then I heard something that made the feathers on the back of my neck stand on end. It was a high, shrill scream, not unlike the shriek of a hawk on the hunt, but about a million times louder and a million times scarier. I ducked my head into the tail feathers of the chicken standing in front of me and we all squished ourselves against the side of a wall. We didn't dare peek through the porch slats and see what was making that unearthly noise. Finally, I decided that one of us had to be brave, so I lifted my head and opened my eyes to look through the porch lattice. That's when I saw the Yankee's secret weapon.

My first sight of him is forever engraved in my memory. Weeks after that day, the whole town would be talking about the mascot the 8th Wisconsin Volunteer Infantry Regiment brought with them into battle. Folks said his name was Old Abe. Old Abe was an eagle, but most folks called him the "Yankee buzzard" and some even spit after saying it. Though folks sure do like to tell the story of Old Abe, most of them never saw him in action like we did. For all my days I will never forget the sound of his scream.

The soldier carrying him ran right past our porch. He was perched high up on a pole with a shield attached. His left leg had a leather strap that kept him tethered to the perch. At first, I thought he was a hawk. Hawks are the most feared of all chicken predators because they soar down from the sky and by the time you see the shadow, it's too late. But this creature was bigger than a hawk, much bigger. He had a white head and a wingspan almost longer across than the water trough our cows drink from. I remembered the stories my mystery used to read to his young son about dragons that breathe fire and destroy whole villages. I didn't see any fire coming from his mouth, but that scream he made was enough to cause me to tremble in fear.

Though I knew I would pay for it with nightmares for the rest of my life, I couldn't help but watch that monster as his mister ran the pole to the front of the line. With every cannon shot, that bird would stretch out his wings and flap. He would screech and dance on his perch excitedly, joining in the battle with his only weapon- his voice. I heard a Confederate general holler at his men, "Blow that Yankee Buzzard to pieces!" The men turned their guns on the bird and fired. He stretched his wings out as if to hit the bullets to the ground. One bullet flew just underneath the bones of his outstretched wing taking

119

off three of his huge flight feathers, leaving a wide gap that somehow made him look even more menacing. Another bullet hit his perch, severing the leather strap from the wood- and that's when the dragon began to fly.

I couldn't help myself, I squawked in terror when he leaped off his perch and swooped down as if to pluck a hapless soldier off the ground with his sharp, pointed talons. He flew low, over the heads of the men on the front lines, shrieking as he went. I closed my eyes and hoped with all my might that he wasn't heading for our porch.

The fight raged on for all that day and the next. We ended up losing the battle of Corinth, probably because of Old Abe. I heard later that he survived and was restored to his perch so he could go on to terrorize some other poor soldiers in other battles. They said Old Abe was named for the president of the United States. I've seen pictures of Abraham Lincoln in old newspapers my mister throws away and he doesn't look anything like that bird.

In the days that followed the battle, our house was used as a makeshift hospital. My missus and mister tended to the wounded, both Confederate and Yankee. There were so many that they laid several Yankee soldiers on the porch above our heads. As I listened to those Yankees talk, I was surprised. They didn't seem like horrible people, I could hear pain in their voices, I could also hear hope when they talked about home and their loved ones left behind. They talked about the same sort of things that my mister and missus talked about. I even got to the point where I forgot they were Yankees. It made me wonder about this war. If we were so alike, why would we fight each other like we did? Neighbor against neighbor, brother against brother. Then I remembered that eagle and how scared I was when he got free and flew down the line. Maybe he wasn't flying because he wanted to attack, maybe he was flying simply because he was free. Maybe this war isn't about bossing people around or deciding who should be in charge of who. Maybe it's about something as simple as freedom. The freedom to scratch in your own backyard without anyone telling you you can't. The freedom to eat a worm you worked so hard to get and not have to give it to someone else who didn't work for it. The freedom to be safe on the roost at night and know that your loved ones will still be perching there next to you in the morning. As much as I hate this war, if it ends with everyone getting to be free, then maybe, just maybe, it will be worth it.

Freedom Comes to Texas, Galveston, Texas, 1871

My mister and missus are pastors. They have a pretty, little church not far from the water. Behind the church they have a house to live in and behind that there is a barn for us. I'm excited because tomorrow is our Jubilee Day. Jubilee Day is very important for a lot of different reasons. Chickens like Jubilee Day because there's a big barbeque and picnic and we get a lot of handouts. Folks like it because it's the day they celebrate when freedom came to Texas. Apparently, for the longest time, folks in Texas were free but they just didn't know it. It wasn't until a mister named Major General Granger came here to Galveston and read a paper telling everyone that they were free, that they finally knew it was true.

Tonight, the folks will gather in the church for a service where they'll sing and pray and talk about freedom. I hope they'll talk about the feast tomorrow too, I'd like to know what I have to look forward to. Right now, I'm staking out my place under one of the tables that have been set up for the lunch. It's important to find the best spot where I can possibly get a lot of scraps that have fallen to the ground. I've chosen a place where two tables meet, that means extra people can sit there and extra bits and pieces can fall off the table. I hope someone has made potato salad, I love potato salad.

It's getting to be evening so I should head into the coop and start to get settled down for the night, but since I'm very upset about something that happened this afternoon, I've decided to stay out here, under the table, and take a dust bath to try and calm down.

Today was the worst day of my life and all because of a blackberry pie.

Blackberries are one of my most favorite things. The sea air makes the bushes grow fast and we always have tons of blackberries to hunt for and munch on in the summertime. When I heard my missus was making blackberries into a pie, I could hardly wait.

While I waited for that pie to be done, I decided to get a head start on dinner. I headed out behind the barn because there's an old, rotted log back there and I knew if I put a little bit of work into my scratching I could round up some termites, centipedes, and even some beetles. I like the shiny kind of beetle that looks blue and green when the sunshine hits it just right. Having a lot of different colors for dinner means your meal is healthy. Well, I was so busy hunting around that I didn't even know that the pie was done already,

When my missus makes a pie she puts it on the windowsill to cool and then gets to doing her daily chores like laundry and sweeping. From what I heard, while that pie was cooling, a whole army of ants marched right up the side of our house and into that pie. I can't blame the ants, blackberry pie is hard to resist. When my missus finally got around to checking on that pie, it was full up with ants. That's when she decided to toss it to the chickens. I don't know why she did that, having ants mixed in with those soft blackberries would have given that pie an extra crunch and some added protein. Now that I think of it, it's possible she invited those ants on purpose because it was always her plan to make a special Jubilee pie for us chickens. She's nice like that. At any rate, as soon as she dumped that pie out on the grass every chicken on our place swarmed it and got a delicious bite or two. Every chicken except me.

By the time I came casually strolling out from behind the barn most of that pie was gone. I let out a squawk and ran full speed to the spot where the pie had been thrown. The blackberry-stained grass still had quite a few chickens pecking around in it. I rushed and pushed my way to the middle, desperate. I would have settled for a small, trampled ant with some blackberry juice smeared on it- anything would have made me feel better. But when I got there, the big, older hens pecked me and chased me. I'm a small hen and not very brave, it was easy for them to push me away. I tried many times to get a taste and suffered the pecks of those grouchy old chickens for my trouble. By the time everyone finally walked away, not a crumb remained. Not a blade of grass. Not even an ant.

So now I sit here under the table, thinking of what could have been. I missed out on that pie simply because I didn't know it was there, and when I did find out, others prevented me from getting even the smallest taste. As I was thinking of this I listened to my mister, the pastor, talking to the church folks about Jubilee Day. I began to realize how it must have felt for folks to miss out on freedom for no reason other than they just didn't know they were free. My mister pointed out that the slave owners knew they were wrong, they knew that the slaves should be free, but they kept that from them just so they could make them work longer. That's when my mister told everyone that Jubilee Day is about freedom, but it's also about forgiveness. I didn't like hearing that, I didn't want to forgive those hens for stealing my chance at blackberry pie happiness.

As the ocean breeze wafted under the table and stirred up some extra dust for my bath, my mister started telling a story about a man who was in bad need of forgiveness. This man had been the captain of a slave ship. He sailed to Africa and stole people away from their homes and locked them up on his ship to bring them to America to be slaves. I thought of that for a moment. What would it be like to be forced away from my home and everything I knew and be taken far away to work hard in a lonely place? I don't think I would like that at all.

My mister went on to say that one night there was a terrible storm on the ocean and that evil man thought he was going to die. He called out to God and asked for God to show him mercy, and God heard his cry and saved him, body and soul. Later on in life that man dedicated his life to telling others about what God had done for him, and he did that by writing a song.

My mister stopped talking then and I heard the church folks start singing the most beautiful song I ever heard:

Amazing grace! How sweet the sound
That saved a wretch like me!
I once was lost, but now am found;
Was blind, but now I see.

'Twas grace that taught my heart to fear,
And grace my fears relieved;
How precious did that grace appear
The hour I first believed!

Through many dangers, toils and snares,
I have already come;
'Tis grace hath brought me safe thus far,
And grace will lead me home.

I'm not sure what all those words mean, chickens don't have a big vocabulary, but I think that man wrote that song because he realized that he got forgiveness from God, even though he didn't deserve it. Maybe that's what my mister was talking about. The word grace means to forgive someone who doesn't deserve to be forgiven. And if we can do that, then maybe God will forgive us too.

As the sun started to set over Galveston Bay, I stood up and shook all that dirt out of my feathers and walked out from under the table clean. I decided to forgive those hens who wouldn't share that pie with me. That was the right thing to do. I turned and headed towards the barn, I needed to get some rest because tomorrow would be Jubilee Day and even though I missed out on that pie, I didn't want to miss out on any of the other wonderful things that the day would bring.

By the Same Author

A Chicken Was There:

Tales of the Pioneer Chickens Who
Helped Settle the Great American West

From Jesse James to Buffalo Bill, from Westward Expansion to the Pony Express, the chickens who were eyewitnesses to history tell their stories in this collection of twenty-five short stories of the Great American West.

A Chicken was There Too:

Tales of the Colonial Chickens Who
Were There at the Birth of America

From Benjamin Franklin to Paul Revere, from the Mayflower to Valley Forge, the chickens who were there at the birth of America tell their stories. Twenty-five short stories take the reader from the early explorers of America through the patriots of the Revolutionary War.

About the Author

Arlene Davenport left a life of battling traffic in the big city for a life of watching the sunset in rural Texas. When she's not teaching junior high English, she spends her time reading, writing, gardening, and trying to survive the Texas heat. She lives in a small town south of Austin with her husband, two dogs, a cat, and fourteen chickens.